a Line of Duty novel

PROTECTING
What's His

a Line of Duty novel

PROTECTING
What's His

#1 *NEW YORK TIMES* BESTSELLING AUTHOR
TESSA BAILEY

This book is a work of fiction. Names, characters, places, and incidents are the product of the author's imagination or are used fictitiously. Any resemblance to actual events, locales, or persons, living or dead, is coincidental.

Copyright © 2013 by Tessa Bailey. All rights reserved, including the right to reproduce, distribute, or transmit in any form or by any means. For information regarding subsidiary rights, please contact the Publisher.

Entangled Publishing, LLC
644 Shrewsbury Commons Ave
STE 181
Shrewsbury, PA 17361
rights@entangledpublishing.com

Brazen is an imprint of Entangled Publishing, LLC.

Edited by Heather Howland
Cover design by LJ Anderson/Mayhem Cover Creations

Manufactured in the United States of America

First Edition February 2013

For Patrick and Mackenzie.

Chapter One

To steal or not to steal, that was the question.

Ginger Peet contemplated the bottle blonde sprawled across the yellowing love seat before returning her attention to the gaping purse full of cash in the woman's hands. Lips pinched, she waited for the proverbial angel/devil tag team to pop up on her shoulders to dole out conflicting advice.

Nothing happened. And didn't that just figure?

Instead, her conscience wiggled out of her chest, moseyed across the room, and perched itself on the giant, unused stereo system circa 1992. It crossed its arms and shrugged as if to say, "Union break. You understand."

Ginger cocked an eyebrow. It appeared her imagination was already overcompensating for the absence of her conscience.

She plopped down on the dingy carpet, pulled her knees up to her chest, and inhaled a shaky breath. Her night shift at Bobby's Hideaway had been crazy as usual, what with the dueling bachelorette parties and frat guys from Vanderbilt screaming drink orders at her until 4:00 a.m. Typical night in downtown Nashville.

Most nights, she screamed right along with them. Playing the part. Laughing at jokes she couldn't even hear above the honky-tonk music. Giving as good as she got. Was it pure coincidence that tonight, when she'd been unable to muster a single smile for her good ol' boy regulars, she came home to find a pile of cash waiting for her?

Furthermore, their mother hadn't darkened their door in months, but had picked tonight of all nights to stop by and catch a nap. The last time Ginger spoke—okay *argued*—with Valerie, she'd been stripping to make a living. If you called passing through life in a drug- and alcohol-induced haze *living*. At least she'd managed to pass out with dignity and not wake Ginger's seventeen-year-old sister, Willa, in the process. Willa tried valiantly to hide her depression over their mother's habitual absences, but Ginger knew it cut her deeply.

Ginger didn't take kindly to anyone hurting her sister. Mother or not.

She narrowed her gaze once more at the cash-filled purse. No way had Valerie pulled in this much cash twirling around a pole. She sifted through the bulging rolls of hundred-dollar bills held together by rubber bands. What she wouldn't give to have this much money. The pile of cash in front of her represented freedom. Change. A chance to pursue something other than pouring drinks to support herself and Willa.

Willa.

This could be Ginger's one and only chance to get her sister away from this broken-down heap called a house. Away from the danger of the strange men her mother brought home when she actually *came* home. Away from the fate of ending up passed out on a thrift-store couch while your twenty-three-year-old daughter debated ripping you off.

And. Yet. Ginger knew with absolute certainty that

if she took this money, just walked out the door with it, it would come back to take a chunk out of her ass. Moreover, it occurred to her that this one poor decision moved her one giant step closer to her biggest fear.

Becoming her mother.

Ginger had to believe the pile of skin and bones on the couch had once possessed dreams and ambitions of some sort. Then one misguided choice landed her in a G-string and pasties shaking it for some trucker named Dirk to a played-out eighties anthem.

If Ginger could just be a *good enough* person for *long enough*, she could flip the script for Willa, though. Willa, who'd skipped the sixth grade, swore like a sailor, and took photographs that could make Ginger cry, would have a chance at becoming something. Someone.

She glanced around at the peeling paint, stained carpet, and twice-pawned television set. Without the responsibility of playing parent to her sister, Ginger would have lit out a long time ago, leaving Nashville in her rearview mirror. The thought of falling asleep in her squeaky twin bed in the room she shared with Willa, only to wake up tomorrow and complete the same bleak routine—riding the bus into town to work a double shift, then still struggle to put dinner on the table *and* make rent, all the while looking out for her sister—made her feel nauseated.

I can't see past tomorrow anymore and that ain't good.

As her idol Dolly Parton once said, "If you don't like the road you're walking, start paving another one." Hell, she was going to need a fleet of cement mixers.

And for that, she'd need some cash.

Ginger fanned the money in front of her face, inhaling the musty scent. Surely the guilt would appear any moment and she would stuff the purse back into the crook of Valerie's arm and pretend she'd never seen it in the first place. She could then fall asleep with a clear conscience and the false hope that her mother had turned over a new leaf and would use the money to feed Willa, move her sister into a nicer home.

Or she could seize the opportunity fate was dropping in her lap and get the heck out of Dodge…

As Ginger picked up the purse and slung it over her shoulder, she learned something very important about human nature. Oftentimes people make questionable decisions. And even though they already taste the fat regret sandwich headed their way, they do it with a smile.

She gave her trembling, wide-eyed conscience the finger and went to pack.

Chapter Two

From his position above the bathroom sink, Lieutenant Derek Tyler stared into bloodshot eyes. *Oh, right. That's why I don't drink whiskey on an empty stomach.*

Derek didn't appreciate the reminder of his own stupidity, nor did he have time to reflect on it. He had under an hour to make it to Saint Luke Cemetery, so he quickly tossed back three extra-strength pain relievers and adjusted the tie of his wrinkle-free uniform.

Chicago PD would bury one of its own today. One of *his* own. Hence his drinking binge the prior evening. Derek had never lost a man in the line of duty before, and that he'd lost one in last week's raid on Chicago's most dangerous crime syndicate burned in his stomach like battery acid.

Unlike Derek, the officer had a family. A family with whom Derek would come face-to-face in under an hour.

As a homicide cop, he knew the likelihood of similar tragedies occurring more than once on his watch was high, especially since he'd only recently turned thirty and had a long career ahead of him. He hoped he never got used to it.

He'd just left the bathroom to retrieve his uniform hat from the closet when his ears were assaulted by high-pitched laughter from outside the apartment building. Derek frowned. He'd specifically chosen this building, a sprawling brick colonial in Hyde Park, for its distance from the constant activity downtown. He preferred the quiet. Especially today, when he felt like an ice pick was firmly lodged in his skull.

"Pick up the end! I can't carry the whole thing, skunk-vag!"

"Fuck off! You're only using one hand!"

"That's because I'm using the other one to flip you off."

"Well, I can't argue with multitasking."

"You would argue with the pope's mom."

Christ. These girls, whoever they were, could give the rowdy men in his department a run for their money. Too bad he didn't allow his men to swear while on duty.

Did he just hear one of them call the other *donkey-queef*?

Derek ground his head against the wall to suppress the pounding in his frontal lobe. He would never drink whiskey again. Normally, the Chicago Cubs were his only vice and that usually proved punishment enough.

With a curse, he strode toward the open window in his sparsely and functionally decorated living room. Thanks to the demands of his job, he spent very little time at home and a couch, television set, and neatly ordered desk completed the space.

From his vantage point at the window, Derek caught sight of a teenage girl pulling a lava lamp from the bed of a rusty, flatbed pickup truck. Her thick black hair hung down well past her shoulders, obscuring his view of her face. Black knee-high combat boots were laced up over purple fishnet stockings.

Judging by the furniture and household items lining the sidewalk, these girls who could curse a blue streak were moving in. The one female he could see certainly did not fit the building demographic. Most of the residents worked in town and kept reliable hours. No loud music or parties. He wondered how these two managed to slip through the cracks.

Unable to connect the second voice to its owner, he started to turn back into the apartment—

The black-haired menace leaned on the truck's horn, startling a scream out of the second girl and causing Derek to smack his head against the window frame. The ice pick in his skull twisted and he literally saw stars winking behind his eyelids.

Before he could stop himself, Derek opened the window and barked in his sternest lieutenant voice, "Hey! Not everyone needs to be in on your moving day adventure!"

All chatter ceased from below. With a satisfied grunt, he slammed the window, scooped up his hat and keys, and headed for the door. His apartment was located on the second floor, down at the end of a long hallway, and as he locked his door, he noticed the apartment across the hall from his stood empty. The door had been propped open by a giant porcelain statue of a blond woman with massive breasts.

Dear God, please don't tell me...

"Move to your *other* left, you crackhead!"

"Ow. *Ow!* Put it down. My hand is falling off."

He turned to find the horn-wailing, black-haired menace staggering down the hall under the weight of what appeared to be a dining room table, looking half-perturbed, half-amused.

Derek's attention swung to the girl carrying the other end of the table, walking backward toward him. He couldn't see her face, but he was immediately riveted by the most beautiful ass he'd ever seen.

Wearing jeans so low-cut they should be illegal, the girl had long, perfectly formed legs that were stuffed into brown leather cowboy boots, immediately searing the image of her riding him like a mechanical horse onto his brain.

Please, please don't let me be getting a hard-on for a teenage girl. Be legal, at least, so I can sleep tonight knowing I'm not a raging pervert.

Derek very nearly had a coronary as she bent over to set down the table and purple lace peeked out over the waistband of her painted-on jeans. His mouth went dry, his vision blurred, and both his hat and keys dropped to the floor.

Surprised by the sudden noise, the girls jumped and yelped, the girl in cowboy boots spinning to face him. And holy hell, if Derek thought he'd been in trouble seeing her from behind, he'd just blasted past the DANGER: ROAD ENDS AHEAD sign and was hurtling over the cliff.

At least I'll die happy.

Her cloud of chestnut-colored hair flipped over her shoulder as she turned to face him and he was lost. Bright hazel eyes, almost golden in color, landed on him and narrowed over high cheekbones. Pouty lips pursed in displeasure. A sprinkling of freckles dusted her nose, making her a cross between sex goddess and girl next door.

An apparently dangerous combination if Derek's reaction to her counted as any indication.

Against his better judgment, he allowed his gaze to dip for exactly three seconds to her flat stomach and tease of cleavage above the tight white tank top she wore. An inch of skin lay exposed above her waistband and in that brief moment, he wanted to drop to his knees and open-mouth kiss that spot below her belly button with an intensity that rattled him.

She was sex incarnate and moving into the apartment across the hall. The situation felt suspicious, like someone was playing a joke on the poor, hungover cop, and if he could manage to look away from her for long enough to check, certainly he'd find a camera crew waiting to let him in on the prank.

He knew in that moment that his peaceful existence had been shattered. With her living across the hall from his formerly quiet respite from work, he'd be forced to walk past her door each day, knowing exactly what lay on the other side.

His eyes landed once more on easily the most striking face he'd ever seen. She arched a single eyebrow at his blatant ogling. Derek decided it had been worth it.

"Did that asshole upstairs actually call the cops on us?"

As he watched those fantasy lips move, revealing a hot little country twang, he drew a blank. Then the situation came back into sharp focus. He stood there in full police department regalia because he'd be attending a funeral this afternoon. And she thought he was there for a noise complaint.

Guilt and irritation swept through him. She'd distracted him at a time when he should be thinking about his fallen officer. How selfish could he be? A man lay dead and all he could think about was dragging Ms. Low-Rider Jeans inside his apartment to assuage the growing ache in his pants.

Pull yourself together, Tyler.

"I *am* that asshole from upstairs."

Chapter Three

Well, dang. They'd gone and moved in right across the hall from a cop. A *hot* cop, if you liked the whole uptight, sexually repressed vibe he had going on. And she'd just called him an asshole. Perfect.

Personally, she didn't care for the belligerence on his freshly shaven face or the way he stripped her bare in one sweep of his dark green eyes. Someone should clue him in that a smile never hurt when you were looking at someone like you wanted them for dinner.

Sorry, but I'm not looking to lend you this particular cup of sugar, neighbor.

Still, she could certainly do *much* worse if she was so inclined. His uniform jacket did nothing to hide his broad chest and powerful build. This was the kind of man who could pick you up and throw you over his shoulder with very little effort, although the sensual tilt of his upper lip contradicted his overall ruggedness. With that steady gaze of his, he practically radiated physical awareness, as if conscious of his obvious appeal, but disinclined to use it.

Should she be worried about living across from a cop? A young, stand-too-close-and-you-might-get-burned cop at that? No, Ginger decided right away. Despite the circumstances surrounding their departure from Nashville, she knew alerting the cops would be the last course of action Valerie would consider. If she knew her mother, that money hadn't been come by legally, and explaining where it came from to the police would definitely cramp her style. Valerie's relationship with the boys in blue tended to be hostile, at best.

No, she had nothing to worry about from this man. Unless she counted the way his heated inspection of her belly button made her toes curl in her boots.

Ginger put a little steel in her spine, refusing the urge to shield herself from his interested gaze, then frowned, wondering why Officer Needs-a-Nap elicited such an odd reaction from her. She'd never shied away from being checked out before, having accepted at a young age that men liked the look and shape of her face and body. A fat lot of good it had ever done her.

But then his eyes snapped up to hers. And determinedly stayed there.

Interesting.

She flashed him her best smile. "Sorry to disturb you, Officer. We didn't think there'd be anyone at home, being that it's the middle of the day and all."

"Well, here I am. And it's Lieutenant."

Ouch. She shoots, she misses. Ginger could practically feel Willa's sarcastic *oh, you don't say!* expression aimed squarely at the lieutenant even though her back was turned to her sister. Ginger was having a difficult time keeping the same expression off her own face. If her teeth were slightly clenched behind her smile, surely Lieutenant Cranky Pants didn't notice.

"My apologies, *Lieutenant*," she countered stiffly. "And

that's my second and final apology for the day."

Ginger gave him her back once more to lift the end of the table, catching a hint of amusement on his face as she turned. Not that she gave a damn.

The cell phone in her front pocket vibrated for the umpteenth time today. She knew who called and why. She also knew she wouldn't answer, or listen to the subsequent voice mail message. First chance she got, she'd cancel the plan and get new cell phones for herself and Willa.

With a nod in her sister's direction, they picked up the table with the intention of continuing into the apartment.

"What the hell is that?"

Ginger dropped the table and faced the questioning lieutenant, making Willa shout a four-letter expletive at the ceiling. His annoyed green gaze flicked to Willa before inclining his head toward the statue propping open the door.

Both she and Willa looked toward the statue, then back at him.

Ginger answered slowly, as if speaking to the town idiot who also happened to be hard of hearing. "I assume you meant, '*Who* the hell is that?' and to that question I say, who are *you*? Who are any of us?"

"I don't follow."

"That, *Lieutenant*, is the Smoky Mountain Songbird herself."

"The Backwoods Barbie," Willa chimed in angrily.

The man looked completely confused, so Ginger decided to take pity on him. "Dolly Parton."

"Dolly *motherfucking* Parton."

"Language, Willa. Honestly."

Ginger waited for a reaction and felt far from satisfied when he merely shrugged his broad shoulders as if to say, "Should I know who that is?"

And that was the final straw.

"Willa, darling, you mind waiting for me inside the apartment?"

She felt rather than saw her sister's eye roll, but heard her comply noisily, stomping inside the apartment. Then Ginger stood alone in the brightly lit hall with the scowling Lieutenant Von A-hole.

Twice he'd made her apologize after *blatantly* giving her the once-over, shot her little sister a dirty look, and then shrugged, *shrugged* at the mention of the Queen of Nashville. And this was *after* he'd yelled at them like a lunatic from his upstairs window.

Ginger couldn't let it stand.

She sauntered forward, coming to a stop a foot away from his tall frame, and had the satisfaction of watching his eyes narrow warily. Up close, she saw his green eyes were rimmed with red and recognized a hangover when she saw one. Having skimmed his starched, navy blue uniform all the way up to his ruthlessly shorn, dark brown hair, something told her *tying one on* wasn't something he did on a regular basis. No, despite his overtly masculine appearance, his reserve suggested he would be the type to order a glass of milk at the bar.

That offended her as a bartender *and* as a recreational drinker.

She took a deep, calming breath and let it out slowly. This morning, she'd woken up happy and optimistic. Ginger couldn't remember the last time that was the case. She'd outrun the storm cloud darkening the sky above her head in Nashville and had come to Chicago for a new start. For her. For Willa. Adios leaky roof and questionable future.

After spending a week in a cheap, dingy motel, Ginger finally found an affordable neighborhood with a good high school nearby, close enough to downtown Chicago and potential work for herself. Then she'd sweet-talked the landlord into a double security deposit in lieu of the mandatory credit check. And bam! They now had themselves a sweet two-bedroom with *new appliances* and *hardwood floors*. Amenities that up until yesterday sounded like a foreign language. She and Willa had picked out furniture at thrift stores and yard sales throughout the week, pretending to be college students living off-campus. They'd had *fun*, dammit. Without a time limit.

And this son of a bitch was raining on their parade.

"What exactly is your problem, Lieutenant?"

He took a step forward, bringing them toe-to-toe, forcing her to look up if she wanted to meet his eyes. *Damn*, this guy kept surprising her. Men liked Ginger. That wasn't arrogance talking. Okay, maybe a little, but it was mainly an observation. *This* man, however, seemed determined to piss her off good.

She couldn't help the smile that spread across her face.

"You can stop calling me 'Lieutenant' now. It's getting on my nerves."

"I believe that was the point."

A muscle in his jaw flexed. "It's Derek from now on."

Oh, he had balls making demands. She'd give him that. "I don't believe I'll have cause to call you anything at all. What do you think of that?"

He didn't answer her question. "I assume there's some sort of parental supervision moving in with you?"

Her smile disappeared right quick. "Beg pardon?"

Derek gestured with the patented cop-head-nod to the open door Willa had recently disappeared through. "She's barely old enough to operate a vehicle and *surely* you're not much older."

Ginger's left eye twitched. This little *tête-à-tête* had just gone from interesting to insufferable. Judging from his stoic expression, he had no idea what kind of land mine he'd just stepped on. Well, he was about to find the hell out. "I'm twenty-three years old, *actually*. And last time I checked, that's old enough to vote, drink, gamble, rent an apartment, own a firearm, and explain to a grown man, police *lieutenant* or not, when he's being a gigantic *dickhead*. And Derek, if it wasn't clear enough already, *you* are the dickhead in this little scenario." She paused for a breath. "And don't call me surely."

His eyes narrowed even further, completely obscuring the green of his irises. "Did you just quote *Airplane!* to me?"

Ginger swore she could feel steam coming out of her ears. "That's really all you picked up on? Glossed right over the dickhead part?"

"What's your name?"

She gritted her teeth. "Hardly matters at this point, wouldn't you agree? I don't think there are too many neighborly chats in our future."

Willa picked that moment to holler from inside the apartment. "Ginger! I'm fucking starving and all we have is Triscuit crackers and strawberry frosting!"

Ah, impeccable timing as usual, sis.

Not quite suppressing his triumphant smile, Derek answered her rhetorical question. "I'd have to agree with you, *Ginger*. I'm not feeling the least bit neighborly toward you."

"Well then, sugar, I'd say our association ends here."

"I doubt that."

"You can doubt anything if you think about it long enough. And I am done thinking about this. Good-bye, Derek. Can't say it was a pleasure, but it was definitely an experience."

Ginger spun around on the heel of her boot with the intention of storming into her apartment, leaving him staring after her, hopefully slack-jawed and regretful. Instead, she ran smack into the dining room table still blocking the hallway, effectively knocking the wind out of her stomach and her sails. Fighting the need to simultaneously suck in deep gulps of air and karate chop the table, Ginger straightened and skirted the table silently, refusing to turn around and gauge his reaction to her embarrassing mishap.

As she closed the apartment door behind her, she heard Derek call to her. "Aren't Gingers usually redheads?"

"Go to hell!"

In spite of the masculine laughter passing by her door, she heard Willa approach. "Well, Ginger, looks like we finally found the one man unwilling to grovel at your feet."

Guess they'd just have to see about that, wouldn't they?

Chapter Four

"All right, Alvarez. Lean harder on your informant. We need to know if anyone has been in contact with the head of the Modesto crew since Monday."

As the detective jumped up and left the briefing room, Derek addressed the remaining assembled detectives and officers. "The streets are too quiet. I think we all know that's when they're most dangerous. We need a heavy presence on the South Side, especially in Back of the Yards. Continue to canvass for witnesses who aren't too scared to talk. Shop owners who've been made victims themselves are probably our best bet. Leave no one out."

He turned his attention to his former partner, who had remained a detective when Derek was promoted to lieutenant two years prior. "Kenny, take Barker and pay another visit to Hector Modesto's girlfriend. She knows where he is—it's just a matter of getting her to talk. Find motivation and use it."

Derek glanced at the giant whiteboard containing mug shots and surveillance photos of the major players and victims of Chicago's latest gang war. His gut told him they'd be adding more photos to the victim side if his department failed to bring in Modesto soon.

He clapped his hands together once. "Get to work."

Immediately, chairs scraped back and the men began speaking, strategizing. He pushed through the glass door and entered his office. Barker, a rookie, followed him in. Cocky and outspoken, Barker had yet to learn anything about boundaries.

"Lieutenant Tyler."

"Help you, Barker?"

"You going to the charity event Saturday night?"

Fuck. He'd completely forgotten, and rightly so. Being in the middle of a turf war between two powerful gangs had kept him working brutal hours for weeks. Politicians, however, organized parties and charity events at their convenience, and as head of the department, his attendance was usually expected. This particular event, raising money for an after-school program in Chicago's worst neighborhood, would be completely different, thanks to Barker. His uncle sat on the city council, which had bought the entire homicide division invitations. They'd all get to dress up in monkey suits and eat shrimp cocktail when they should be working.

"Don't have much of a choice. Why?"

"Just checking. My uncle wants to bend your ear a little."

"Great. Is that all?"

"Yeah." But for once the young officer looked uncomfortable. "I hate to bother you with this trivial bullshit, but no one in my uncle's office has been able to get you on the phone."

Barker had fallen silent. "I'm waiting."

"You RSVP'd for two." Derek turned his eyes to the ceiling and Barker rushed on. "My uncle had no problem paying for the extra plate since a lot of the guys are bringing dates…but the men say you usually fly solo…"

True. Mixing work and his personal life wasn't something he typically allowed. Introducing a woman to his closest colleagues tended to give her false hope that the relationship would move forward, when it rarely did. Women wanted him to play the hero after hours, but once he clocked out for the evening, he had little interest in being nice. In the end, the women he dated usually found his tastes too intense for their liking.

Derek vaguely recalled handing the invitation to Patty, the department's soon-to-be-retired dispatch operator and unofficial personal assistant, asking her to respond on his behalf. She'd either put him down to bring a date on accident, or she was playing one of her notorious pranks on him. Derek supposed he could show up on his own, blaming Patty for the mistake. Then again, these charity dinners charged upward of one thousand dollars per plate. He couldn't very well let a councilman foot the bill for nothing. Keeping politicians happy, annoying as it happened to be, remained in his best interest.

"Tell them I'm bringing someone."

"What's her name?"

"Why do they need to know that?"

Barker gulped. "The place card for the table."

"Jesus." Derek ran an impatient hand over his hair. "I'll let you know."

As Barker beat a quick path to the exit, Derek leaned back in his chair, allowing the heated meeting with Ginger in the hallway to play through his mind again, as it had done frequently since that morning, three days prior. Each time, he remembered something different about their encounter. Her floral scent, the smooth line of her throat, that damn sexy accent.

She claimed to be raising her seventeen-year-old sister. He couldn't think of many women in their early twenties capable of shouldering that type of responsibility. It was a distinct possibility that she hadn't been given a choice. The need to know more about Ginger ate at him...and he didn't understand why. Despite his obvious attraction to her, this insatiable curiosity over a woman was damned unusual for him.

After a brief hesitation, Derek typed "Peet, Ginger" into the search bar of the national database. He'd learned her last name this morning after seeing it on the building mailbox assigned to her apartment. Based on her accent, Derek narrowed down his search to the Southeast section of the country.

He stilled in his chair when a two-week-old missing person's report popped up out of Nashville, filed by a Valerie Peet, also listing Willa Peet, a minor, as missing.

It gave little information about the circumstances surrounding their disappearance, but color photographs had been provided by the mother, one being Ginger as a teenager. Willa's appeared to be a recent school yearbook photograph. Neither one of the girls had police records.

He stared at Ginger's photo. Though undeniably beautiful, she looked too thin and tired, appearing surprised that someone cared enough to take her picture. Shaking off a frisson of unease, Derek returned to the search screen and typed in "Peet, Valerie, Nashville."

Her rap sheet took up the entire screen, including reckless endangerment of minors, crystal meth and prescription drug possession, public intoxication, prostitution, and a handful of DUIs. He could spend all day combing through the charges, but he was mostly interested in the first.

Derek clicked the first reckless endangerment file, dating back to 1999. As he read the description of Valerie's criminal charges, he grew more incensed with each detail. A ten-year-old Ginger had been brought into a Nashville police department for attempting to shoplift food to feed four-year-old Willa. She told the officer their mother hadn't been home since Christmas, two weeks prior.

Based on her latest charges, dated as recently as four months ago, Valerie hadn't changed since leaving her two young children to starve all those years ago. Ginger had been seeing to Willa's welfare for quite some time, it seemed. How they'd avoided being taken into state's custody, Derek couldn't fathom.

Something about the missing person's report niggled at his detective's brain. Why would Valerie Peet, a woman who obviously had very little use for her children, even bother making the effort to report them missing? Furthermore, after years of neglect, what would prompt Ginger to take Willa and leave Nashville only a couple of months before Willa graduated high school?

Derek had no way of finding out. Thanks to his massive hangover and annoyance over finding himself lusting after a woman on his way to a funeral, he'd made a less-than-stellar first impression. He very well couldn't knock on her door and pry into her personal business when it shouldn't be his concern in the first place.

The part that scared the hell out of him?

He wanted to make it his concern.

Chapter Five

Ginger used her trusty pink scissors to cut out the headline Is Your Vagina Angry? from a newly purchased women's magazine, spread glue on the back, and pasted it over the picture of a nun looking thoughtful. She had a sick sense of humor. So sue her.

She stepped back and admired the decoupage nightstand she'd been working on all day. *Get Thee to a Nunnery*, she'd named this particular one. After a few finishing touches, it would be ready for a coat of lacquer.

Ginger smiled. Her hobby of decorating various pieces of furniture with interesting photographs and magazine cutouts might have started as a way to occupy her mind when living in Nashville, but somewhere along the line, she'd started doing it for fun. Since she purchased most of the furniture at donation centers, the expense was minimal, and creating something one-of-a-kind brought her a sense of accomplishment. Occasionally, she'd even sold pieces to students or visiting artists she met at Bobby's Hideaway, although such a thing proved a rarity since the clientele didn't have much interest in discussing furniture. Any money she'd made went into a college account for Willa. In a bank where Valerie couldn't touch it.

She sighed into her half-empty wineglass, knowing her free time would be limited from here on out. While Willa attended her first day at the new high school, Ginger went out and found a job bartending at Sensation, a nightclub in the River North section of downtown Chicago.

Old habits die hard, she supposed. Bartending felt like a step backward after the progress she'd made leaving Nashville behind last week, but money came easy behind the bar. And if she knew how to accomplish one thing, it was getting people good and trashed. With the money she'd "borrowed," Ginger probably didn't need to work for quite a while, but apart from using some of the cash as their security deposit on the apartment, she didn't plan to touch it unless absolutely necessary.

Ginger glided into the kitchen, taking a moment to appreciate the marble countertops and stainless steel appliances. She couldn't get over living with such luxuries. Just last week she'd been reheating three-day-old leftovers over an ancient gas stove. Today, Willa would sit down to homemade pasta sauce and ravioli. The ravioli itself was store-bought, but hey, she'd never claimed to be a chef.

A door slammed out in the hallway and Ginger smirked, assuming the lieutenant must be home from work for the night. Not once had she thought about him since their exchange the other day. Unless you count that one time. And the fourteen other times he'd popped into her head, damn him.

Maybe Chicago boys just liked something a little different in a woman.

Like hell.

She couldn't recall a time when a man had intentionally

pushed her buttons so effectively. Apart from his initial head-to-toe appraisal, Derek genuinely hadn't seemed all that interested. It shouldn't bother her so much, but it did. Damn him, it did.

Their apartment door slammed next, making Ginger jump and splash marinara sauce onto the counter. She quickly wiped it up with a dish towel.

"Heck of an entrance, Wip." It was the nickname she'd given Willa while she'd still been in diapers. Willa Ingrid Peet. Wip for short.

"I try."

Ginger glanced over her shoulder, smiling at Willa's black Misfits T-shirt and ripped stockings. Somehow Willa managed to pull off the look. "How'd it go? Did you refrain from setting the place on fire?"

"Just barely. I'm choosing my moment."

"Well. Don't forget your lighter fluid or it won't take."

"Noted."

She gestured with her wineglass. "Go drop your stuff off in your room. Dinner's almost ready."

Ignoring Ginger's instructions, Willa dropped her book bag on the floor and climbed onto the countertop behind Ginger, who merely shook her head. Willa did as Willa pleased. "This all feels freakishly normal. I don't know if I like it yet."

Ginger hummed in understanding but didn't turn around. "I reckon we'll get used to it," she said quietly, spooning fragrant sauce into bowls on top of the cooked ravioli. "I got a job today. Starts tomorrow night at seven."

"No shit. Doing what?"

Ginger paused, avoiding Willa's eyes. "You know, the usual. Bartending."

Watching Ginger closely, Willa took a bite. "You cool with that?"

"Yeah! This place is amazing. Real swanky." She changed the subject, knowing Willa would be forced to follow suit. Her sister had always been too perceptive. "How's the pasta?"

"Not bad for store-bought."

"Oh, jump up my ass."

Fifteen too-quiet minutes later, after they'd finished dinner and she'd helped with the cleanup, Willa disappeared into her room to begin working on her homework.

Ginger had always made a point, even in Nashville, to sit down and share a proper dinner with Willa. Even if the meal consisted of creamed corn and toast, their family meals were a constant. Something they both counted on to mark the passing of time. They weren't required to speak about their day or remark on the weather, but Willa had been quieter than usual tonight.

Had she been wrong to bring Willa here? She knew her sister encountered bullies on occasion, but assumed tough-as-nails Willa let that type of thing roll off her back. Maybe she'd been wrong and Chicago was a new kind of animal her sister couldn't handle.

The thought weighed heavily on her mind. Ginger resolved to pry the truth out of Willa tomorrow at dinner, whether it upset her or not.

After placing the final magazine cutout, a large pair of lips with legs, on the nightstand, Ginger coated the project with lacquer and made a mental note to seek out local flea markets in Chicago where she could purchase a vendor space to sell the pieces once she accumulated a decent stock. People had liked her designs in the past. The idea that she might make money by selling them wasn't so far-fetched, right?

Ginger poured herself a second glass of wine, then glanced at the clock, surprised to see the early hour. At a loss over what to do with the rest of her night, the landlord's mention of a roof garden on top of the building popped into her head. She called an invitation through Willa's closed door, but got no response, so she wandered out of the apartment and up the staircase by herself. When she reached the top floor, Ginger pushed open the heavy metal door leading to the roof.

Wow.

From this vantage point, she could see the glittering lights of downtown Chicago and the bright beacon that was Wrigley Field. The night felt cool against her mostly bare skin, and she took a deep, fortifying breath, letting it out slowly. A jolt of surprise shot through her when she registered a familiar scent she couldn't quite place. Sort of like leather and expensive coffee.

Her eyes flew open. Derek, arms crossed, leaned against the wall enclosing the rooftop. Watching her.

Damn, he looked just as good in jeans and a sweatshirt as he did in that navy blue uniform. And it annoyed the bejesus out of her. She couldn't decide from his bored expression whether or not he appreciated her intrusion, and after a minute decided she didn't give a damn. Derek didn't own exclusive rights to the roof, even if his posture suggested he might.

The last thing he said to her yesterday about Gingers usually being redheads popped into her mind. Oh, he wouldn't win this round. She'd make sure of it.

Smiling, Ginger put a little swagger in her step and approached him.

...

Derek struggled not to show a reaction to the feminine temptation walking—*sauntering,* really—in his direction. Before she'd caught sight of him, he'd watched, hypnotized, as she let her head tip up toward the sky and shook that hair back over her shoulders, sighing through those bee-stung lips.

He'd hardened painfully upon hearing the sound, capturing the sigh of contentment in his memory bank. She would sigh for him one day. But he'd only allow it after making her beg for—and then scream—her release.

Like a living thing, the swift and potent possessiveness she provoked in him stretched and vibrated in his belly. He'd wanted women before, but not like this. He wanted Ginger *immediately*. To do things to her he'd only ever fantasized about. If another man had happened to be present on the roof at that moment, Derek didn't doubt he'd throw the unlucky bastard over the side before letting him get a glimpse of her lithe body.

Rein yourself in, Tyler. The last time he'd seen the woman, she'd cursed him to eternal damnation. If he wanted to get anywhere near her, he needed to first make sure she could stand the sight of him.

Derek didn't normally come up to the roof. Nothing to accomplish up here. But the thought of her less than ten yards away, cooking dinner and humming to herself, had driven him out of his own apartment to escape the torturous mental pictures. Ginger licking sauce off her fingers. Ginger bending over to take something out of the oven. He couldn't take it one second longer.

Now, she'd followed him onto the roof, and if her seductive walk and determined expression were any indication, his suffering had only just begun.

Stopping within reaching distance, Ginger tilted her head and extended the wineglass she was holding. "Peace offering, Lieutenant?"

Fuck. That accent made him want to put her over his knee just to hear the kinds of things she'd say as he spanked her exquisite ass.

Harder, darlin'.

Giving himself a mental shake, he eyed her outstretched hand. "Wine is a woman's drink."

"Humor me."

He hesitated—he wouldn't put it past her to poison him after their first encounter—but Derek finally took the glass and drank deeply, watching her over the glass rim, then handed it back.

"Well, now that we've ruled out wine, what exactly is your drink of choice, Derek?"

He liked her saying his name way too goddamn much. "Why do you want to know?"

She shrugged. "You can learn a lot about somebody by what they drink. Wine drinkers are usually sentimental and artistic. They like to tell stories. Light beer is for younger men and women on perpetual diets. Dark ales tend to attract the adventurous. Martinis are for women looking to feel sexy." She sent him a feline smile. "So which one are you, Lieutenant?"

"Whiskey. Neat."

Derek savored the pleasure of watching surprise spread across her face. "Really? Interesting."

"What did you think it would be?"

"Milk."

"Milk?"

"Mmm-hmm. Although, funny enough, some people do refer to whiskey as *mother's milk*. So technically I was right." She took a congratulatory sip of wine. "Whiskey drinkers are no-nonsense folks. They don't take time to enjoy the process of getting drunk. It's all about the end result for them."

"I'd have to say that's accurate." He dragged his gaze up from her mouth. "Some things I like to take my time with, though."

Her eyes widened a little, as if he'd caught her off guard with that comment. Derek decided he could really make a habit of shocking her. Rubbing her arms, she turned and walked away, stopping a short distance from him to look out at the city view. Derek recognized the perfect opportunity to excuse himself and go back to his apartment, but instead he found himself following Ginger across the roof.

"You have a lot of experience with alcohol," he said from beside her.

Ginger confirmed with a distant nod. "Been bartending too long, I suppose."

He could only imagine the way men fantasized about the possibility of taking her home with them as she poured and served their drinks. Especially considering the way Ginger tended to dress. Drunken assholes probably stood five deep at the bar just to get a glimpse of her passing by.

Unconsciously, his fist clenched at his side.

"Do you work in town?" Even to his own ears, his voice sounded strained, and he watched her eyes narrow trying to interpret his tone.

"As a matter of fact, I just got hired this afternoon at Sensation up on West Kinzie."

Derek didn't recognize the name, but she sounded less than thrilled over her new employment. Judging by the location, the clientele would likely be young people looking to get laid. Everything about this situation annoyed him. "Where did you work before?"

"Oh, you wouldn't know it," she said quickly, making his built-in avoidance detector chirp. She obviously didn't want him knowing where she'd come from.

"With that accent, you're obviously not from Chicago."

Ginger took a sip of her wine without replying, although he supposed it hadn't exactly been a question, more of a statement. Based on their interactions so far, Derek didn't foresee her appeasing his curiosity any time soon. And yeah, he was curious as hell. But he needed to remember they weren't sitting in an interrogation room. However, if they were, now would be the time to play "good cop" if he wanted to get anywhere with Ginger.

"Listen, I'm sorry about the other day. You caught me on a bad morning."

Ginger cocked her hip and turned to face him fully, the wind plastering her tissue-thin dress against her curves. Light pink silk molded to her breasts like a second skin. He could even make out a distinct outline of the lacy bra she wore underneath and absently wondered how easily the material would rip in his hands.

"You mean, you don't make a habit of antagonizing your neighbors? If you tell me you're actually a member of the welcoming committee, I won't believe you."

He chuckled. "No, I don't normally antagonize my neighbors. In fact, I barely speak to them at all."

"Oh, so we just got lucky, then."

"You have a funny way of accepting an apology." He watched Ginger sip her wine. "I was on my way to a funeral. Colleague of mine. So, yeah. Bad morning."

All traces of humor drained from her expression, the base of her wineglass clinking down on the concrete wall surrounding the roof. "I'm so sorry."

Derek shrugged, surprised by the sincerity on her face. "Don't be. I just wanted to explain." Wanting to move past the seriousness of the moment, he added, "What about you? I seem to remember someone calling me a dickhead and telling me exactly where to go."

Flipping her hair back over her shoulder, she smiled up at him. His breath got trapped in his lungs. *Damn*, this girl knew exactly what she was doing.

"Now, Lieutenant. It's not very gentlemanly to remind a lady of her past transgressions."

"I'm having a very difficult time remembering to be a

gentleman around you."

Her smile wavered a little bit. Was it his imagination or did he have as much effect on her as she did on him? Impossible, he decided. While there might be some attraction on her end, nothing could compare to the single-minded lust he was experiencing. It was quite literally all he could do not to throw her over his shoulder and carry her to bed right then and there.

Easy, boy. If he allowed even a hint of what he was thinking to show on his face, he'd scare her away. He needed to keep it together.

"Well, if you're not a gentleman, maybe I shouldn't be up here alone with you on a dark, deserted roof."

Despite her words, Derek detected a hint of breathlessness in her voice and felt the answering tug low in his belly. If she'd given any indication that he intimidated her, he would've pulled back, but that didn't appear to be the case. No, she seemed...*interested.*

His hooded eyes dropped to her sassy breasts and watched her nipples stiffen against the thin fabric before dragging his gaze back up to hers. Definitely interested. The part of him that usually alarmed women started to rear its head. He gave her one final out.

"Maybe you *shouldn't* be up here with me, Ginger."

Her breathing kicked up a notch. Excitement moved through him as he waited to see what she'd do. Draining her wineglass in one long swallow, she met his eyes. "Maybe I like it up here."

Closing the distance between them, Derek tipped her chin up in his hand so he could look down into her considerably wound-up expression. He would be taking a risk, but decided to lay all his cards on the table anyway. What he had to say might shock and disgust her. But if it didn't, if she found his words gratifying, the reward would be sweet. God, what he wouldn't give to voice his needs for once without judgment or falsely coy reactions. Ginger's approval seemed especially vital.

"I warned you that I'm having a difficult time being a gentleman. Should I assume you're provoking me on purpose?"

She wet her lips. "Is that what I'm doing?"

The need to kiss her inundated him, but he wouldn't give in to it until she asked. Derek rubbed the pad of his thumb across her plump bottom lip, pleased when she inhaled sharply but didn't pull away. "Let *me* be clear, Ginger, since you insist on talking in circles. I want you underneath me in my bed. I want to be buried inside you so deep that I have to remind you of your own name. And I want those motherfuckers leering at you from the other side of the bar to smell me on you for a week afterward."

Her eyes widened with each declaration. She opened her mouth to speak but nothing came out.

"I just wanted to be up-front. Good night, Ginger."

Forcing himself to remove his hand and step back lest he push her too far too soon, Derek turned and descended the stairs to suffer alone in his apartment.

Chapter Six

Ginger set two bottles of light beer on the bar, smiling playfully up at the stocky grad student in a backward Bulls hat. Without taking her eyes off him, she swayed to the cash register and made change for his twenty-dollar bill. "You kiss your mother with that mouth, sugar?"

"No, but I'd love to kiss you with it."

Not a chance in hell, but if you leave me a nice tip, I'll let you think it's a possibility.

Ginger set his change on the bar and laughed. "Now, there's an offer I might consider."

His slightly drunker friend nudged him with an elbow and raised his eyebrows, clearly approving of Backward Hat's boldness. Ginger cringed. Not that they didn't appear to be fine, upstanding young men, but tomorrow they'd wake up with hangovers and either be embarrassed or have forgotten this whole exchange. Or maybe they'd take their girlfriends shopping at the mall, winking at each other when tonight came up in conversation.

"Can I get your number?"

She pulled a sad face. "Sorry, darlin'. I can't give my number out while I'm working. But if you give me yours, I just might decide to use it."

Backward Hat high-fived his friend like Ginger wasn't standing three feet away, then grabbed a napkin from the plastic holder. He drunkenly scrawled his name and number on one side and slid it across the bar. *Matt.* She stuffed it in her back pocket along with the two other napkins with numbers on them she'd been given tonight. They'd be perfect for her current project. A decoupage trash can decorated with men's phone numbers. Symbolic.

Backward Hat Matt. Kind of a rat. Since we've been chatting, your beer has gone flat.

"You better call me!" Matt said, picking up his drink and disappearing back into the crowd.

Ginger sighed and moved on to the next customers. Thankfully, they had vaginas. While shaking their martinis in a silver shaker, she acknowledged her luck in finding this job. Although the night's tips hadn't yet been counted, she'd easily pulled in double what she made working in Nashville.

Sensation stood in a hip part of town with many other bars and nightclubs. With two floors of pumping dance music and three separate bars, college students and young professionals flocked to the establishment every night of the week. Wanting to test her skills, the manager had placed Ginger on the first-floor bar, closest to the entrance where the flow of traffic never ceased, for which she felt grateful. Tonight had been meant as a training shift, but her new coworker Amanda quickly recognized Ginger's experience and left to work the other side of the bar. The time flew by and the money rolled in.

Looking up from the martinis she artfully strained into chilled glasses, Ginger smiled at the approaching Amanda. Also in her early twenties, Amanda sported a blond pixie cut that Ginger found daring and perfect for her angular face.

Her new coworker had to shout over the music to be heard. "Hey! Looks like you got the hang of everything quick!"

Ginger responded in kind. "Everything is so well-organized all I have to do is make drinks. I've been so busy, I don't think I've stopped for a second!"

She leaned in closer and winked. "That's because all the men have been favoring your side of the bar."

Ginger gave her a dubious look. "Oh, come on now. Wasn't that you I saw doing tequila shots with those businessmen about ten minutes ago?"

"I'm sure I don't know what you're referring to."

Ginger laughed and set down napkins in front of the group of girls on which to place their martinis. "Don't worry, I won't tell. Tequila shots are sacred among my kind."

"Good to know. Listen, you've got one more admirer on my end that wants you to serve him. There were no spots available on your side of the bar."

Frowning, she tried to look past Amanda, but couldn't make out distinct faces at the other end of the darkened bar. Who would be demanding her service? She hadn't been in town long enough to make any friends.

"You want to take my side for a while?"

"Sure. Go ahead and serve him." She hip-bumped Ginger, urging her on. "Honestly, I'm a little jealous. He's all kinds of hot and smolder-y. Keep thy wits about ye."

With a laugh, Ginger made her way to the other end of the long bar, gauging drink levels of the customers as she passed. After pausing to fill two orders, she finally made it to the end and saw him.

Derek.

His eyes bored into her, making her feel naked where she stood. The way he sat, exuding quiet confidence, made him stand out amid the animated scene taking place around him.

A slow roll of heat eased its way through her. Goose bumps broke out along her arms. In the brief moment that she met his eyes, the music faded and they were back on the roof. Just her and him. Except this time, he kissed her.

Giving herself a mental shake, Ginger released his unwavering stare to move lower. She'd already seen him in a uniform and then jeans and a sweatshirt, but Ginger pegged this look as her definite favorite. A black T-shirt stretched across his chest, the right sleeve just high enough to show a tattoo peeking out underneath the material. Stubble darkened the lower half of his face, as if he hadn't shaved since this morning.

He looked dangerous and sexy. And pissed.

She refused to let him rattle her. His parting words on the roof last night had echoed in her head at the strangest times today, making her itchy. Of all the men who'd attempted to pick her up in this lifetime, never had one made it beneath her skin. She didn't like the feeling.

Much.

Ginger grabbed a tumbler from the clear glass shelf and poured two fingers of their best whiskey.

"Are you here to issue more warnings?" she asked, sliding the drink in front of him.

Keeping his gaze locked on her, Derek picked up the glass and drank a healthy mouthful. Ginger swayed a little watching his throat muscles work as he swallowed, then set the glass down. "No. I think I was abundantly clear the first time."

His answer reminded her of a whip cracking. "Something bothering you, Derek?"

"How are you getting home tonight?"

She smirked at his nonresponse to her question. "I took the bus."

"I'll drive you."

"Thanks for the offer, but I'll take my chances with public transportation."

He swirled the amber contents of his glass. "Can't handle being alone with me?"

Damn. There he went again pushing her buttons. She claimed to be a smart girl, but he still knew just how to play her, didn't he? Ginger always had a difficult time backing down from a challenge, especially when it was being issued by a man who wore a police uniform by day, but liked to talk dirty at night. She found his approach refreshing. He'd explained what he wanted, plain and simple.

A part of herself she hadn't known existed until yesterday came alive. She *wanted* to be alone with him. To hear what he'd say next. To see exactly how he hoped to accomplish his goal of getting her into bed. A man hadn't tempted her in a long time, and never this way. Never this strongly.

I want to be buried inside you so deep that I have to remind you of your own name.

Ginger shivered at the memory.

"I get off in an hour. If you don't mind waiting…?"

A fire lit in his eyes. "I'll wait."

For the next hour, Ginger remained on Derek's end of the bar serving the finally thinning crowd. Men continued to flirt with her and she didn't allow Derek's presence to prevent her from flirting back. She had a living to make, after all. Without looking at him, she knew he continued to watch her. His constant regard burned her up, made her feel feverish. Heaviness settled between her legs and she grew increasingly damp, making it difficult to concentrate on work.

In retaliation for the discomfort he was putting her through, Ginger began leaning a little too far across the bar to hear someone's order or exposing a little more stomach than necessary to reach something on the higher shelves. The uniform worn by the bartenders at Sensation consisted of tiny black shorts and matching halter top. Even with Ginger's penchant for dressing to distract, the outfit left very little to the imagination.

Still, he'd occupied her thoughts more than she felt comfortable admitting and he would suffer for it, she thought, bending at the waist to pick up a dropped napkin and giving him a nice look at her ass.

Finally, the hour ended and not a moment too soon. Ginger felt ready to expire under Derek's hot scrutiny from the end of the bar. She collected her tips and waved goodbye to Amanda, then held up a finger to let Derek know she would be another minute. As soon as she had her purse, she met him at the entrance.

Wordlessly, he held the door for her leading to the parking lot and walked brusquely to a black SUV. He opened the passenger door, allowing her to slip inside, green eyes on her as she edged past. Derek's leather and coffee scent lingered in the car's interior, and as he rounded the back of the car, she inhaled, committing it to memory.

The ride between Sensation and their apartment building took ten minutes. For the first half of the ride, they both remained silent, but Ginger could almost feel the aggravation radiating from Derek.

"So, tell me. Is bartending the only type of employment you could find?"

Ginger bristled. "There aren't exactly dozens of options where I can bring home the same kind of money. Besides, I'm good at it."

He laughed bitterly. "Oh, believe me, I know how good you are. I just witnessed it firsthand."

"I have Willa to think about. She'll be in college next year and I aim to see her go wherever she wants."

"On a bartender's salary."

His skepticism irked her, but she kept silent. Bringing up the stolen cash would be high on the list of stupid ideas. Ginger knew how expensive college would be and held no illusions that sending Willa would be easy. But she'd see it accomplished nonetheless.

"If you need me to get a job in some lame-ass real estate office just so you feel better about sleeping with me, you're wasting your time, honey. And mine."

His eyes didn't leave the road, but his jaw flexed at her words. "I assume, based on your statement, that you've given some thought to what I proposed last night?"

Jesus, who *talked* like that? "I'm considering it."

"Is there anything I can do to speed you along?"

"I don't know…"

"Think harder."

Turning her face toward the window, Ginger smiled. She'd finally succeeded in rattling him a little for a change. "You're going to have to work for it a little, Derek."

"I'm not exactly a champagne and soft music type of guy."

"Then I guess it's a good thing I like cheap red wine and country music."

Derek pulled into a spot outside the building and Ginger hopped out, intending to bolt inside her apartment and savor the fact that she'd finally gotten in the last word. She made it up the stairs, down the quiet hallway, and to her apartment door before she felt him come up behind her. Suddenly, the keys were snatched from her hand. She spun around in time to see Derek drop them into his pocket.

Her mouth fell open at his audacity. "What are you doing?"

"You can have them back in a minute."

Derek's gravelly tone called several other things into focus. The slight flush of his cheekbones, his roughened breathing, the overwhelming nearness of his hard body. Her back arched against the door, an unconscious move that drew his gaze downward, to where her breasts pressed snugly inside her halter top.

I want him to look at me.

The realization shook her and she swallowed as he took a step closer, her throat suddenly dry. "I thought I told you you needed to work for it."

He leaned down, and his big hands came to rest on either side of her head, mouth stopping a mere inch away from hers. "I think we have two different definitions of what *working for it* means."

"Oh? What's your definition?"

"Do you want to me to tell you?" He brushed his lips along the underside of her jaw. "Or show you?"

The blistering contact of his mouth on her skin sent shock waves coursing through her system. Since meeting, she and Derek had shared two sexually charged encounters, but this moment marked the first time he'd touched her and the effect was like a drug straight to her brain. Her head fell back, inviting him to kiss her in the sensitive spot again, but he remained still, waiting for her answer.

She lifted her head and looked him in the eye. "Show me."

His mouth came down on hers, hard and hungry. The initial contact proved so potent, they both had to pause for a shuddering breath. When she slid her hands up to his shoulders and dug her nails in his flesh, he groaned and lifted her against the door. Desperate to get closer, Ginger's legs came up to circle his waist, and she moaned when Derek pushed against her with his hips, holding her backside in place with rough hands. She broke contact with his mouth, gasping at the hardness pressing against her damp shorts.

"Did you enjoy putting on that little show for me behind the bar?"

One hand left her bottom to travel up, over her hip and rib cage, stopping just under her right breast, eyes piercing hers with a silent question. *Oh, God.* She nodded, and when his palm slid up and over her breast, squeezing gently, her eyelids fluttered closed at the excess of sensations. She could feel him watching her, weighing her every reaction as he ran his thumb back and forth across her hard nipple. The arousal she'd experienced earlier tonight while Derek watched her work exploded with added intensity. A whimper escaped her lips. A sharp ache pulsed between her thighs.

"I asked you a question. *Did you enjoy it?*"

Derek's words deepened the ache beating within her to a painful level. In that moment, she wanted nothing more than for him to whip off her shorts and panties to take her hard and fast against the door. She licked her lips. "Yes."

His eyes flared. "Was your performance for me alone or every man with a goddamn pair of eyes?"

He expected her to *talk* when his mouth was moving to her neck, sucking the sensitive spot underneath her ear? Expert lips traced a path down to her collarbone and back up, and he bit the tender area with a low growl.

"Is it all a tease or do you ever let them take you home?"

Ginger rolled her head to the side, begging for his lips to return to her neck. The hand plastered to her ass kneaded relentlessly, keeping her moving against his erection with intensifying friction. If he would just let her move her hips a little, she would come, even with her shorts on, but his hand and hips controlled her every action. She made a sound of frustration.

His breath rasped out harshly against her ear, punctuated by each thrust that pinned her to the shaking door. Knowing she affected him so powerfully in return made her dizzy. When his mouth found hers once more, she bit his lower lip then licked it, meeting his eyes under heavy lids. He responded by devouring her mouth on a loud groan, sucking her tongue until she writhed against him.

When Derek abruptly ceased his calculated torture, Ginger protested, seeking his mouth once more. He resisted.

Levering her against the door, he ran skilled hands down her thighs and hooked his arms under her knees, pulling them up until they almost reached his shoulders. Then his hips pressed in and upward. Hitting her right where she needed it. Ginger's head fell back against the door.

"*Derek.*"

"Answer me."

She couldn't remember the question. Her breath raced through her lips. Release hovered just within her reach. "No! I don't go home with *any* of them. Ever."

Her sincere answer appeared to calm him somewhat, but then he stepped back, dropped her legs and let her slide down his body. They both groaned at the contact. Ginger wanted to cry with frustration and nearly did so, but then the reality of their situation hit her full force. She'd been two seconds from letting a near-stranger screw her in a public hallway. Although this type of reckless behavior was out of character for her, it eerily reminded her of something. Some*one*.

Her mother.

Bitter anger and shame swept through her. Pushing against Derek's chest, she let him see the full force of her fury. "And after that performance, what the hell makes you any different from the drunken assholes at the bar? You're exactly like them. The only difference is I had the bad fortune of moving in across from you."

His momentary calm evaporated and he backed her once more against the door, grasping her chin in his hand. "The difference is, you don't want any of those men to fuck you. But you want me to fuck you very badly. Don't you, Ginger?"

"No."

Laughing darkly, one big hand dropped between her legs. He palmed her mound and squeezed, then ran two seeking fingers along the seam of her shorts where the telltale wetness gave her away. "Liar."

"I hate you."

His eyes narrowed dangerously. "Would you like me to prove what a liar you are?"

"No, I'd like you to give me my keys so I can get the hell away from *you*."

She snatched the keys from his outstretched hand and unlocked the door. Once inside, she threw the deadbolt and leaned back against the door, breathing heavily through her nose.

A moment later she heard heavy footsteps move down the hall.

Sinking down onto the floor, Ginger quickly realized three things.

One: She'd completely underestimated the effect Derek had on her. He possessed the ability to make her completely forget everything but him. The effect he had on her body. Valerie had forgotten herself one too many times and Ginger wouldn't follow suit. No way in hell.

Two: He'd somehow stolen the phone numbers from her back pocket without her knowledge.

Three: She needed a vibrator. A powerful one.

Chapter Seven

Derek stared at the files on his laptop screen, unease settling over him. He hadn't been able to shake the feeling there was more to Ginger leaving Nashville than a neglectful mother, and now that he'd done a little more digging, it appeared his intuition might be right. According to Valerie's most recent possession charge, she'd been bailed out of jail by an H. Devon. He'd quickly searched the name in the Nashville area.

In addition to a hefty rap sheet of his own, Haywood Devon owned several strip clubs in the Nashville area. Suspicion of drug trafficking and prostitution inside his clubs looked like it kept the Nashville police department on Devon's doorstep every few weeks.

If Haywood Devon was the type of character Ginger's mother associated with on a regular basis, he didn't doubt she'd been afraid of more than a missed meal. Men like Devon didn't bail anyone out of jail without expecting a favor in return. When those favors didn't come through, the families of his debtors paid the price.

Two familiar voices drifted up to him from outside the

window. Derek closed his laptop and watched Ginger and her sister hop out of their beaten-up, rusted orange pickup truck, and collect the paper grocery bags from its flatbed. Willa yelled something—obscene, no doubt—to Ginger over the back of the truck, and Ginger threw her head back in unrestrained laughter.

Derek's stomach muscles went rigid at the sight of her. Walking through the doors of that ridiculous meat market last night, he'd sat down at the bar with every intention of engaging her in a normal conversation for once. One that didn't end with both of them pissed off. Then he'd been forced to watch for over an hour as she fluttered her eyelashes and flaunted her body, giving every man within a hundred yards, including him, a hard-on that could cut through steel.

Possessiveness, insistent and primitive, had flowed through him like lava. Once they got back to their building, his plan had been to drive Ginger to the brink of orgasm and back off, leaving her as frustrated as he'd been watching her seduce the crowd at Sensation. Instead, he'd lost control, had come too close to fucking things up, and the knowledge sat like a weight in his stomach. He never lost control. Deciding to indulge himself had always been a conscious decision on his part, never an undeniable need, demanding to be met.

Then again, Ginger was the first woman he'd come across who bred such strong feelings in him. Derek couldn't even guarantee the next time they found themselves alone would be any different. His reaction to her didn't appear to be something he could control.

But the more he thought about it, the more he suspected restraint wasn't the way to go with Ginger. She'd liked the way he spoke to her—*goddamn* that excited him—and she'd responded to his loss of control with an equally potent explosion of passion and need of her own. Recalling the way she'd wrapped her agile body around his like ivy, digging those sexy cowboy boots into his ass, made Derek groan aloud in his silent apartment.

She'd tasted like melted caramel, as if she'd been sucking on hard candy. And damn if those hot little whimpering noises she'd made against his ear hadn't kept him awake all night.

As the object of his frustration and her little sister passed his door on their way to their apartment, Derek sighed. *You're going to have to work for it a little*, she'd said last night. So he would try, with her definition in mind. But he'd make her work for it as well. Giving away the upper hand was not something Derek did under any circumstance.

He grabbed his keys and left his apartment.

• • •

Willa shoved a plastic sack of carrots into the refrigerator's vegetable drawer, kicking it shut with her heavy boot.

Ginger visibly cringed. "Did you misplace your opposable thumbs, Willa? Jeez."

Her sister looked thoughtful. "I may have left them in the produce aisle. Can I borrow the car to go get them?"

Ginger snorted a laugh. "As long as you have your middle fingers, you'll survive. And I don't think you can refer to the contraption we're driving as a *car*. Steel death trap, *yes*. Truck, *maybe*. Car, *no*."

"The General has never failed us. He's a classic."

"A classic piece of shit," Ginger quipped, sticking a box of frozen lasagna in the freezer. "So," she began casually, "three days of school so far. How's it going?"

"Fine. I, uh, have to go to this stupid basketball game on Friday night for a photography class project."

Willa was opening up to her? Ginger strove for nonchalance. "You're attending an actual sporting event?

Careful you don't burst into flames at the entrance."

As usual, they both laughed on cue, but Ginger saw the shadow that clouded Willa's expression. "I didn't mean anything by that," she said quickly. "It's just, you know...you're pretty outspoken about your hatred of organized rituals."

"No, you're right." Her sister smiled. "I better call ahead to make sure they have a fire extinguisher handy."

Something about her tone was still off. "Willa—"

A knock sounded at the door.

They both frowned. Willa made it to the door before Ginger could stop her, opening it a mere crack with the chain lock still in place. "State your business."

A beat of silence. "Is there an *adult* at home?"

Ginger's heart sped up at the sound of Derek's deep timbre. What on earth could he be doing at their door? They may have practically had sex in the hallway last night, but that didn't mean they had a cordial, "howdy neighbor" relationship.

She pasted a bored expression on her face, strode to the door, and unhooked the chain, opening the door to reveal him fully. Once again, he looked good enough to eat in a long-sleeved, gray thermal shirt and dark jeans. A silver badge was clipped to his belt.

"Can we help you, Lieutenant?"

His green eyes flickered lazily over her body, then back up to meet her eyes. "I think we know each other well enough by now to be on a first-name basis."

She ignored Willa's confused expression and sent Derek a sharp look. "If you insist, *Derek*. We are neighbors after all."

"I do insist."

"Well, then."

"Are you guys trying to eye fuck each other to death? If so, can I *please* be excused?"

"*Willa!*"

Derek let out a deep, booming laugh. Willa rolled her eyes at Ginger's horrified expression.

She whipped her head back around to a still-laughing Derek. "Is there something you need? I'm just about to cook dinner and then I'm heading out to work."

His laughter faded at the mention of her job, but instead of commenting he held up a plastic bag she hadn't noticed. "Don't bother cooking. I brought Chinese." Then he breezed past them into the apartment, leaving them gaping at his broad back.

Willa recovered first with a very uncharacteristic squeal. "Chinese! Thank God."

Ginger stared dumbfounded as Derek and Willa began unloading white and red cartons from the plastic bag and placing them on the dining table. "Wait a minute. I'd planned on cooking chicken potpies. You love my potpies. Don't you?"

"Oh honey, you know I love *everything* you make." The *honey* gave her sister away. She'd never been the endearment type. And when had she started liking Chinese food?

Ginger sniffed, then followed them into the kitchen. "You could have said something," she muttered as she yanked plates out of the cabinet. "Here I am now looking like a big potpie-peddling jackass."

As they spooned spicy honey shrimp and orange chicken onto their plates, Ginger watched Derek warily across the table. He caught her staring and raised a questioning eyebrow. The man was clearly up to something and as soon as she caught him alone for a minute, she'd make him spill it. Until then, if he wanted to pretend this heartwarming little scene passed as normal, she'd go right along with it. "So, Derek. Tell us more about being a police lieutenant. It sounds so dangerous!"

He narrowed his eyes at her caustic tone, but answered

anyway. "I work in the homicide division. It can be dangerous, yes, but it's mostly lots of dead bodies."

Ginger choked on a bite of egg roll and took a long sip of water to recover. Fortunately, the mention of dead bodies appeared to pique Willa's interest.

"Do any of them ever wake up and scare the shit out of you?"

"No."

"Do you have a catch phrase?"

Derek snorted. "No."

Willa looked disappointed, but seemed to console herself with a cream-cheese-filled wanton.

"Is there a particular case you're working on right now?" Ginger asked.

"Yes, actually. Two rival gangs have been taking each other out one member at a time. I'm tempted to let it continue since that would eventually solve the problem, but that's not my job."

Ginger looked at Derek with fresh eyes. He was too young to sound so cold. Earlier at the door he'd laughed, genuine humor temporarily replacing his usual stoicism. For that brief moment, he'd seemed free of his harsh responsibilities, but now his serious mask lay firmly in place once more.

"I read this article once about gang initiations. Some pretty scary stuff," Willa commented. "Usually it's robbing a convenience store or something, but other times new members have to take out a rival. Could that be what's going on?

"You seem awfully interested." Derek leaned back in his chair, eyeing her sister's hair and clothes. "You thinking of starting up a gang of aspiring morticians or something?"

"*Derek!*" Ginger admonished, ready to jump across the table and strangle him. No one, save herself, insulted her sister and lived to tell the tale.

Willa's mouth dropped open at the insult, but instead of

impaling the good lieutenant with her chopsticks, she threw back her head and laughed.

Ginger had finally seen it all. Her sister making normal conversation, then laughing uproariously with a stranger. Something was definitely in the Chicago tap water.

"Not bad, Lieutenant Lo Mein. Not bad at all."

Derek went back to eating without commenting on his new nickname, but Willa had apparently only gotten started. Ginger popped a dumpling into her mouth and leaned back to watch the show.

"Since you've earned my grudging respect *and* put a hilarious vision in my head of pasty, leather-clad gang members in dog collars roaming the streets, I feel you've earned the right to some helpful knowledge. *And* since you've come here on a Chinese food pilgrimage with the intention of getting laid—"

Ginger shot forward in her chair. "Willa!"

"—I'm going to take pity on you. My sister doesn't date. You're wasting your time."

Derek raised his eyebrows, looking back and forth between her and Ginger. "Oh? And why is that?"

Alarm bells went off in Ginger's head. "Willa, don't you dare."

Her sister ignored her plea as if she'd never spoken. In fact, Ginger was starting to feel like a spectator at a cage match. "That would be because of a series of incidents we refer to as the 'Holy Trinity.'"

"Actually, it's a really boring story and I don't think Derek wants to hear it."

He smiled at her. "Wrong."

Willa speared a wonton with her chopstick. "Around the time of Ginger's twenty-first birthday, she made the fateful decision to try her hand at dating. What would transpire in just three short days has been widely referred to as the three worst dates in human history. My sister has never *once* made it past the appetizer." Holding up one skull-ring-adorned hand, she began ticking off Ginger's humiliations. Ginger could only press her hands over her face and hang her head in defeat.

"The first man's name was Huey Lewis. No joke and no relation. He casually dropped the fact that he operated a gerbil farm in his basement during predinner drinks. When Ginger laughed since he was *so obviously* pulling her leg, Huey Lewis proved his claim by pulling his pet gerbil, Cooter, out of his coat pocket and depositing him on the table."

Willa ticked off a second finger. "Then there was Bill. Ginger's coworker set them up on a blind date and when Willa showed up at the address he'd given over the phone, she found a church. It turned out to be Ginger's very own ambush baptism. Something new the congregation, all of whom were present, were trying out in an attempt to reach out to the community."

Ginger groaned loudly, then stood up and began shoveling empty food containers into a garbage bag. Anything to avoid the amusement on Derek's face.

"Willa, I really think that's enough. I mean it." She even stamped her booted heel for emphasis.

"Sis, you can't really expect me to leave out Walter the eunuch."

Derek had just taken a sip of water when Willa dropped that bombshell. Her sister had to stand up to pound him on the back until he could breathe normally again. Served him right. If his intentions were to get laid, laughing at tales of her humiliating foray into the dating world was not the way to go about it.

"All right, if everyone is finished amusing themselves at my expense, I have to get ready for work. Surely you have some dead folks to get to, Lieutenant?"

He didn't take the hint. As Willa flopped onto the couch to fiddle with her camera, Derek circled the apartment, inspecting everything from the locks on the windows to her current decoupage project. She'd picked up the oversize wooden treasure chest at a yard sale down the street yesterday and began work immediately, giving it a childhood theme. Upon seeing it, she'd envisioned a child storing his toys inside and it inspired her. Using parenting magazines and children's activity books as her guide, she'd cut out everything from teddy bears to cartoon characters to accomplish the theme.

"What's this?" he asked, nodding toward the chest.

"Decoupage."

Derek raised an eyebrow, prompting her to explain. For some reason, it felt too intimate sharing her hobby with him. If he mocked her for it like he did everything else, she wouldn't know how to react. Her buyers were like-minded people with an appreciation for the creative. Derek probably wouldn't know creative if it bit him on the ass.

She sighed. "I buy used furniture and personalize the pieces with magazine and newspaper cutouts. Like that one over there." Ginger pointed toward the Parisian-themed coffee table she'd completed last week and decided to keep since it suited the apartment.

He walked over to inspect it and Ginger turned to wash a glass in the sink, afraid of seeing judgment on his face.

"It's good. Do you sell them?"

Ginger jumped at his deep voice right behind her in the kitchen. In her peripheral vision, she noticed Willa get up and enter her bedroom, closing the door with a *click* behind her. To give them privacy, no doubt.

Willa seemed full of surprises today.

Ginger turned to him, flipping her hair over her shoulder. "No. I mean, every so often someone back in Nashville would buy one, but it's really more of a hobby." With an inward wince, Ginger realized she'd just revealed where they'd lived prior to Chicago. Volunteering information didn't seem wise considering what had prompted their departure.

"Maybe you should make it more than a hobby."

She felt herself flush a little under his compliment, not used to men commenting on anything beyond her looks. He could have been patronizing her, but it didn't feel like it.

Derek circled the kitchen, eyes lighting on everything in their path, weighing and measuring. She supposed he couldn't simply turn off his ability to observe and analyze after hours, but having him in her house felt strange. Honestly, it would feel strange having *any* man in her house, but Derek in particular kept her off-balance, never knowing what to expect. They'd established a physical attraction and she'd been interested in possibly pursuing it, but Chinese food and bantering with Willa, that felt like something more.

Ginger pushed down the rising panic at that thought and decided it was high time she reestablished some boundaries. This relationship would be strictly physical. She didn't need or want some messy emotional entanglement with anyone.

"Are you looking for something illegal so you'll have an excuse to handcuff me, Derek?"

Derek's eyes darkened as he approached, and a shiver ran down her spine. Oh boy, did her lieutenant ever love dirty talk. She delighted in knowing his weakness. He likely spent all day at work maintaining that resolute control, but around her, the sexually charged bad boy took over.

"Baby, I don't need an excuse to cuff you. I just need the opportunity."

Lordy. He'd managed to get her hot and bothered in two sentences. Maybe her weakness was talking dirty, same as him. Ginger's head tipped back as Derek moved closer, bringing her up against the sink.

"Oh, and just how do you plan on creating such an

opportunity?"

Derek brought his hand up to rub a thumb across her bottom lip. "I've got an hour before I need to be back at the station. I'll have fucked you three different ways by then."

Ginger's breath caught on a gasp. "You certainly don't mince words, Lieutenant."

"I think you love it."

Did she love the indecent way he spoke to her? *Yes.* Should she be offended? *Probably.* But it felt honest, and she couldn't deny the overwhelming effect it had on her body.

"Maybe." Her tongue licked out at the pad of his tracing thumb and Derek groaned. "But I still can't be seduced with a bag of Chinese food. Try harder, Derek."

"Point taken. But one more thing." Derek leaned forward, resting his hands on either side of her on the counter, then dipped his head lower. Ginger's mind reeled as he ran his tongue upward in one long lick of her neck. "The longer it takes me to get between your thighs, the rougher I'm going to be when I finally get there. Understand?"

Her chest rose and fell quickly with stuttered breaths. Trembling with the effort to resist begging him to take her to his apartment and make good on his threat, Ginger nodded.

Just like that, she'd surrendered to him. And it felt fantastic.

One hand slid down her back and palmed her ass, kneading the flesh in a gesture of blatant ownership.

"Be good tonight, Ginger. I'll know if you're not." Then he turned and left the apartment, leaving her staring after him.

It was beginning to become a habit.

Chapter Eight

Ginger stared up at the dark ceiling of her bedroom mentally listing adjectives to describe her current state of mind. "Livid," "violent," and "pure spitting mad" topped the list. Following close behind were "impressed," "bemused," and "slightly turned on."

Tonight's shift at Sensation had been a doozy, to put it mildly. Fifteen minutes after she clocked in, a badge-wearing detective had taken a seat at her half of the bar. Thinking nothing of it, she'd served him a scotch and soda before moving on to the next customer. But by the time an hour had passed, her entire section was filled with jacket-and-tie-wearing detectives laughing and trading battle stories.

At first, Ginger had thought, *well hell, this is damned unusual*. Until she realized that every customer of the male persuasion who approached was being treated to looks of undisguised hostility from the pack of badges clogging the bar, sending him to Amanda's side or to another section of the club. Furthermore, not *one* single detective had looked below her neck or addressed her with anything but polite deference the entire night.

"What brings you to Sensation tonight, boys? We don't get a lot of cops in here unless they're arresting somebody," she'd joked, looking for any hint that might confirm her suspicion that Derek had put them up to it.

They'd exchanged innocent glances before their spokesman responded, "I don't know what you're talking about. We come here all the time."

In a pig's eye. Derek's fingerprints were all over it.

Be good tonight, Ginger. I'll know if you're not.

The only thing, and she meant the *only* thing, saving Derek from a 2:00 a.m. ass-kicking was the fact that they'd tipped Ginger well and sent her home with enough money to cover the loss of her usual penis-toting customers.

Derek's motive for pulling such an obnoxious stunt continued to be the part that stuck in her craw. He couldn't very well send his group of tattletales in to spy on her every night of the week. Therefore his sole motivation had been to toy with her. Let her know what he was capable of. His arrogance clearly knew no bounds.

So why then, when Ginger pictured stomping down the hall to Derek's apartment to give him a piece of her mind, did the scene end with him lifting the hem of her nightshirt and boosting her onto the kitchen counter?

She would be damned lucky if the manager at Sensation hadn't noticed something odd about their new clientele and attributed it to Ginger. They wouldn't appreciate their regular customers being intimidated by Derek's trained dogs. Finding another equally lucrative job would be difficult for her, and a gap in employment would make it necessary to dip in to the stolen cash.

As usual, the reminder of the money made Ginger uneasy. Most of the time, she could pretend it didn't exist. That they'd moved to Chicago without having to steal in order to make it happen. Funny how a group of cops and one seriously overbearing lieutenant could make you a little nervous about some harmless larceny.

She worried that someone willing to go to such extremes to keep an eye on her would have no qualms about delving into her past. Possibly had already done so. Though she was convinced Valerie had come by that money illegally and wouldn't be stupid enough to report it stolen, there were no guarantees in this life. If that information was out there, Derek could find it easily enough.

Ginger flopped over onto her stomach, cramming the pillow underneath her head, and did her best to block the image of Derek's face after learning her dirty little secret. Besides, there were more important things to worry about at present.

Like how to keep her head on straight when Derek seemed determined to knock her off-balance, right into his bed.

And how maybe she wanted him to.

Something wet dripped from the ceiling and landed with a *splat* on Ginger's cheek. Two more fat drops of water plopped on her face, then immediately turned into a steady stream of water, soaking her hair and face.

"What the hell?"

She threw her comforter off the bed and climbed out. In the dim light of the bedside lamp, Ginger saw the growing outline of wetness on the ceiling above her bed. Water fell from several different locations around the room. Her bedclothes, which had been dry only seconds ago, were now sopping wet.

She grabbed her new cell phone off the dresser and pulled up the super's number. Obviously a pipe or something had burst, and he needed to turn off the water to the building before her entire bedroom ended up soaked. She would already have one hell of a time cleaning up the current mess.

She rounded the bed, but just before she reached the door, the entire ceiling collapsed, showering her with even more water and pasty plaster particles.

Ginger stumbled backward and fell to the floor. Scrambling, she reached for the knob to the bedroom door and pulled herself up. She threw one last bewildered look at her room and the veritable waterfall now cascading into it, then ran to Willa's room. "Wip! Wake up!"

Her sister shot straight up and screamed. "Ginger? What the fuck?"

"My ceiling just caved in and there's water everywhere. I want to get you out of here in case it's not just contained to the one room."

Willa gave a doubtful head tilt. "Are you sure you're not dreaming?"

"Look at me. I'm soaked!"

"All right. I'm up."

Cautiously, they entered the living room and flipped on the light to find the ceiling darkening with the spreading water above.

"Oh, God," Willa whispered. "Ginger, your furniture."

She'd been avoiding that side of the room with her eyes, but looked over now to find the child's hope chest she hadn't yet lacquered sat directly under a stream of water, along with two unfinished decorative chairs and several hatboxes.

She blinked back tears. "It's not important."

Willa searched her face for a moment before her eyes shot wide.

"Dolly," they breathed at the same time.

Ginger barely had time to register the perfect synchronicity of their leaps over the waterlogged couch and coffee table. They each grabbed an end of the five-foot-tall Dolly statue and lifted, groaning under its weight. Ginger took the lead, wobbling backward through the wreckage, showing Willa where to step safely. They needed to move quickly. Judging by the rapidly growing stain on the ceiling, standing underneath the wet plaster didn't seem wise.

"Ginger, lift! You're going to knock off one of her boobs if it hits the table!"

Grunting over the strain in her muscles, she lifted Dolly up and over the dining table. "For once I wish Dolly had smaller tits," she panted.

Thankfully, they made it outside without mishap and Ginger managed to get the sleeping super, Lenny, on the phone and up to their apartment in less than two minutes. By that time, their living room ceiling had partially caved in, the room filling rapidly with water. Ginger and Willa were waiting with their Dolly statue in the hallway when he ran up the stairs, still buttoning his jeans.

Lenny took one look in their apartment before sprinting up the stairs to Ginger's upstairs neighbor's apartment. A minute later he sprinted past them again, presumably down to the basement so he could turn off the water. The steady stream flowing into their apartment finally subsided, but Ginger didn't dare go back inside. Instead, she stared through the doorway in silence at the new home they'd barely had time to get used to.

Lenny, looking incredibly stressed and apologetic, explained to them that their upstairs neighbor, a middle-aged woman living alone, had been suffering from the flu and thanks to her cold medicine, had passed out waiting for her bathtub to fill some three hours earlier. The older building's flooring had been no match for the weight of the water, sending it downstairs to Ginger and Willa.

It seemed like only minutes after Ginger's call to Lenny, the fire department arrived to begin pumping out the water and also attend to their upstairs neighbor, whose illness appeared more serious than she'd originally thought.

As she and Willa pressed themselves up against the hallway wall to let the firefighters by, she heard Derek's door slam. He exited the apartment wearing gray sweatpants and a T-shirt, clearly having been woken by the commotion. Narrowed eyes ran over the firefighters walking into her apartment, then landed squarely on her. Until his eyes dipped and ran the length of her body, she'd forgotten her attire consisted solely of a sopping wet white nightshirt. She hastily crossed her arms over her breasts and stepped in front of Willa, who wore a similar shirt. In black, of course.

Glaring at the passing men, Derek stomped back inside his apartment without comment. He returned seconds later carrying two giant fleece sweatshirts with police department logos over the right breast. He tossed one to Willa, who gratefully pulled it over her head, then yanked one over Ginger's head. It fell to her knees.

"What the fuck is going on?" he finally asked.

She and Willa were cold and homeless and this asshole had the nerve to demand answers from her? Fuck that. "Don't bark at me!"

Derek pinched the bridge of his nose and turned to walk into her apartment. A moment later, she heard Lenny relaying the story to Derek, the super's harried voice fading in and out as they surveyed the damage.

"Ginger?"

She looked over at Willa. "Yeah?"

"Does this mean we're going back to Nashville?"

The numbness in her sister's voice made tears prick behind Ginger's eyelids, but she kept them in check. Later, she might cry over how this type of catastrophe seemed to follow them around and wonder if maybe she deserved it. But right now, Willa needed reassurance.

"Girl, it'll be a cold day in hell."

Willa looked hopeful. "Yeah?"

Ginger tilted her head. "You like it here?"

Her sister nodded.

"Then we stay." Nodding her head at the statue, Ginger smiled. "Dolly said once that if you want the rainbow, you've got to put up with the rain."

"How fucking appropriate."

They laughed.

Derek came back out of the apartment then with Lenny and two firemen. His eyes met Ginger's immediately and she swore an apology lurked in there somewhere. Watching the way he communicated with the firefighters and Lenny, asking questions and discussing how long repairs would take, Ginger saw him in yet another light. Derek, the cop, currently stood in front of her in the exact spot she'd also met the moody, uptight neighbor and the filthy-mouthed lady killer.

While she'd been lost in her own thoughts, it appeared they'd come to some important decision, because all four men turned to look at her.

Derek finally spoke up in his no-nonsense lieutenant voice. "All right, let's go. You two are staying with me."

Chapter Nine

"You must be high."

Derek frowned as Ginger's words had the two rookie firefighters behind him snickering under their breath. *Oh yeah? I'd like to see* you *try, assholes.*

Scratch that. He didn't want them trying *anything* with Ginger. He couldn't blink without seeing the way she'd been dressed when he first came out of his apartment, and one look at the guys' faces said they remembered, too. She'd been wearing a soaked white T-shirt that barely covered her ass, and her puckered breasts and red panties had been visible through the thin layer of cotton, baring her to everyone's view. Even now, with her wearing his fleece, Derek remained unsatisfied with her lack of clothing. If rookie number two glanced at her legs one more time, he'd use the man's suspenders to strangle him.

"Don't argue with me about this."

She scoffed. "Oh, this isn't an argument. That implies you might win."

Derek prayed for patience. "Can we have a moment?"

he asked tersely, turning to the other men. They threw final glances over their shoulders at Ginger, setting Derek's teeth on edge, then disappeared back into the apartment.

He stepped forward, reaching for her arm.

"Do *not* touch me, Derek. I will clean your clock."

"Why don't you explain to me what your problem is."

She got right in his face then, looking righteously pissed-off and achingly beautiful, even with damp strands of hair sticking to her neck and face. He wanted to kiss her. "My problem is you *telling* me what we're doing and not *asking*. I make decisions for us. Not you. Your badge has no jurisdiction here. Or in my place of work, for that matter!"

Shit. He'd known that artless move would come back to bite him in the ass. Even if he'd only given his detectives an unprecedented night off with the *suggestion* they try Sensation for a drink or two. The promise to transfer anyone who made a pass at Ginger to a precinct somewhere in Appalachia had merely been implied.

Derek knew the most expedient way to deal with this situation. She would probably hate him for it tonight, maybe even tomorrow. But he'd reached his limit of arguing in the hallway while her legs were exposed for everyone to see. And letting her leave the building wasn't a viable option.

"It's three in the morning. Are you planning on taking Willa out in the cold, soaked head to toe, to find a hotel at this time of night? That would be dangerous and could end up with you or Willa sick."

Over Ginger's shoulder, Willa's eyes widened in horror. "Not cool," she whispered.

Confused by Willa's reaction, Derek's eyes swung back to Ginger. Instead of the anger he expected over his blatant manipulation, her pretty features were stricken with guilt. Derek felt hollow inside just seeing the transformation. Had he actually put that look on her face to avoid a stupid argument?

Ginger turned to face Willa, who looked desperate for the earth to open and swallow her whole. "Of course. I wasn't thinking, Willa. I'm sorry."

The girl was already shaking her head. "Ginger, don't listen to him. We'll do whatever you think is best. You *always* do what's best."

Her smile looked sad. "No, I don't. And he's...right. We'll figure something else out tomorrow, but tonight we'll stay here. With Derek."

Ginger turned to him expectantly, but didn't meet his eyes. At a loss, Derek cleared his throat and gestured for her to precede him down the hallway to his apartment, which she did. As Willa passed, she waved toward the giant statue.

"Be careful with Dolly."

Half an hour later, Derek sank heavily onto the end of his bed and ran irritated hands over his cropped hair. He stripped off his shirt and tossed it in the vicinity of his hamper, then collapsed back onto the mattress with a heavy sigh. The last half hour had been an exercise in frustration, with Ginger refusing to meet his eyes and Willa sending him constant death stares as he showed them to his guest room and gave them linens to make up the queen-size bed. He couldn't shake the feeling he deserved Ginger's cold shoulder, but with her refusal to acknowledge him, there wasn't a hope in hell of getting her to talk.

Deciding sleep would prove impossible tonight, and knowing he was due at work in mere hours anyway, Derek grabbed the laptop off his side table and began scanning through crime scene reports. Halfway through the second one, he heard the bathroom door connecting to the living room open and shut. A minute later, the shower started to run. He tried to focus on work and block the image of Ginger naked twenty yards away, but the sound of muffled sobs drew him up short.

Knowing he might somehow be responsible for those tears mobilized Derek and before he knew it, he'd left his bedroom and stood in front of the bathroom door, rapping gently with his knuckles. The hushed sounds of her crying ceased at the sudden noise.

"Ginger?"

A beat of silence. "Yes?"

Derek sighed at the sound of her hoarse voice. Coming to an important decision, he pushed open the bathroom door without waiting for permission.

Ginger sat perched on the marble counter with her bare legs dangling, looking so impossibly young, his heart clenched. She'd shed his fleece and once again wore only the translucent nightshirt that stopped mid-thigh. Drying hair curled wildly around her face, falling forward to partially obscure her expression.

Then her head whipped toward him, puffy eyes widening at his presence in the bathroom, and her beauty punched him in the gut like an iron fist. Although her shoulders sagged under the weight of whatever had upset her, she somehow retained the stubborn set to her chin, the challenge in her eyes. It humbled him, seeing her like this.

As Derek turned to close the door, he took a moment to gather his scattered thoughts, then moved toward her. When he stood directly in front of Ginger, they watched each other for one long, silent moment before her face crumpled. Without hesitation, he came forward and put his arms around her, holding her tight as she shook. To his utter shock, she wrapped her slight arms around his neck and pulled him closer, sobbing brokenly into his neck.

In Derek's line of work, it was difficult to avoid crying females. They were frequently present at crime scenes. Mothers, wives, daughters of the deceased. He'd hardened himself against it long ago. He wouldn't be able to perform his job otherwise. But every so often, a loved one reached a deeply hidden part of him. A child who'd lost her father, unusually stoic, watching the coroner drive away. A mother, days after her son's murder, still refusing to accept his death. If such tragedies ever left him completely untouched, it would be time to retire.

But as Derek watched himself holding Ginger in the mirror over the sink, her smaller, trembling body engulfed by his naked arms and chest, he felt the furthest thing from unaffected. Every sob or shudder that moved through her robbed him of breath. Derek wanted to decimate her sadness and anything causing it. Feeling powerless, he rubbed circles on her back with one hand.

"I'm not good at this," she mumbled against his neck. He barely heard her over the drone of the still-running shower.

"Good at what, baby?"

Ginger pulled away, wiping her tears away with shaking hands. He let her go, even though he wanted to crush her back to his chest.

"Everything. Being responsible for my sister. Making decisions for us."

"Listen, Ginger, what I said earlier about you taking Willa out in the cold—"

"No. No, that's not it. But it's one example." She took a deep, fortifying breath. "That ceiling would have crushed me to death tonight. Five seconds later, I'd have been a goner and that would've left Willa completely alone in a strange city. Oh God, what was I thinking?"

Certain he'd gone white at her revelation about the ceiling, Derek did his best to talk around the giant knot in his throat. "You couldn't have known the ceiling was going to fall, Ginger."

She shook her head. "You don't understand."

"Help me, then."

"Coming to Chicago was my decision." She scrubbed a hand over her face. "I thought we would be better here. Willa would have more opportunities. But, oh God, I'm in completely over my head, aren't I? I don't know how to repair a flooded apartment or cook a decent potpie or even talk to my sister about what's bothering her. I'm not qualified for any of it."

He stroked her hair out of her face. "Listen to me. You've had a long night so everything seems a little worse than it really is. You and Willa weren't hurt. The rest of it you'll handle, because you don't have a choice. Chicago or some other town, the same problems will follow you."

Ginger choked on a disbelieving laugh. "Jesus. Your bedside manner needs serious work."

"Sorry, but how bad can someone really fuck up a chicken potpie? I'm sure yours are fine."

Laughter bubbled from her throat. "I can't believe I actually feel better after that locker room pep talk. But gee, thanks coach. I guess I'll get back out on the field and show them whose house it is."

"I like a woman who can make a decent sports reference."

"Then get used to disappointment because my career in sports references just peaked at one."

Sighing heavily, she slid off the counter, careful not to touch him. "So, it appears we've well and truly blurred the lines tonight."

"What do you mean?"

"We were working our way up to something, I'm not sure what. But here we are, roommates, and that paints everything in a different light."

His eyebrow quirked up. "Make an attempt to be clear, please."

"*I mean* we can't sleep together now. If we did, you'd

never know if I consented merely because I was grateful for your help. And I'll always wonder if you only invited us to stay to score points and get me into the sack."

"Ginger, are you sure the ceiling didn't hit you on the head tonight?"

Her face showed disapproval. "Now, Lieutenant, it's impolite to discuss my recent upset."

He gave her a look.

"There's only one way to redefine the lines and put us back on equal footing. I'm going to pay you rent until we get back into our apartment. That way, we'll never have to wonder."

"Ginger."

"Wait. I have two rules. No more detectives coming into Sensation and getting in my hair. I've never needed a babysitter before and I sure don't need ten of them now."

God, this woman exasperated him. She stood a foot away from him wearing a transparent T-shirt and panties, oblivious to the danger she was in of being dragged to the floor and fucked into submission, giving him *rules*.

"And the second rule?"

"Huh?"

"You said there were two rules."

She appeared to be deep in thought. "Oh, right. The most important one. No sex until I'm back in my apartment."

He barked out a laugh. "Baby, I'm not sure I can make it five more minutes."

Ginger's mouth dropped open, her wide eyes dropping briefly to the bulge pressing against his sweatpants. "Derek, I'm serious about this. I'm not going to be your live-in booty call."

The hot mist from the unused shower had slowly begun filling the room, making the air around them warm and sticky. Water pelting the bathtub and glass shower door created a constant drumming noise, muting their voices to anyone but each other. It felt incredibly intimate, being half-dressed with her in his bathroom. Seeing her among his things. Hearing the soft hum of her voice through the curling steam.

Her hair, dry when he'd entered the bathroom, had begun curling in the humidity, sticking to her neck and chest, which rose and fell in a shuddering breath upon seeing the look in his eyes. Unerringly, his gaze landed on her taut, pink nipples, visible to him through her clinging nightshirt.

Derek stepped toward Ginger, forcing her back with his body. He kept walking until she sat on the counter once more. Placing his hips between her parted legs, Derek ran his hands slowly up her calves and circled her knees slowly, before gripping her bare thighs.

He spoke directly into her ear. "I don't give a fuck about blurring the lines. You won't see my men at the bar anymore, but that's the only one of your rules I'll concede." She started to argue, but he squeezed her thighs tightly to keep her silent. "I'm not a total bastard, Ginger. I'd already decided tonight wasn't going to happen before I came in here. Otherwise, I'd be pounding an orgasm out of you right now."

Her breath caught and she started squirming restlessly on the counter. Derek knew if he kept talking and pushed a little harder, he could have her here and now. But he wouldn't allow it. She'd hate him afterward for taking advantage of her emotional state and back off permanently. One time with her would not be enough, so that didn't work for him.

But God, her naked body was driving him insane. Derek made the mistake of burying his face in her neck to catch her wildflower scent. Her head dropped back, begging him for more contact, and before he knew it, his mouth opened to kiss and suck her damp skin. Ginger moaned, sliding to the very end of the counter. His survival instincts told him to move back, away from her, but his body ignored reason and moved closer. Naked thighs came up to circle his hips, and then her core was pressing and moving against his erection.

"Sweet fucking hell," he gritted. The thin panties she wore provided almost no barrier between them. He could reach down, rip them off, and be inside her within seconds. He allowed himself one hard thrust against her, startling a cry from her lips, before stepping away. The physical pain he experienced looking at Ginger, half-naked and willing, while in his aroused state nearly broke him.

"Derek, don't do this to me again."

Placing his hands on either side of her waist, his head dropped forward. She was right. He couldn't leave her like this. Not a second time. Even if it might kill him.

Derek roughly pulled Ginger off the counter and turned her around to face the mirror. He yanked her back against his body so she could feel his need for her, then brought her hands up around the back of his neck. The position stretched her body, leaving her completely vulnerable to him.

Derek's hands dropped to the hem of her T-shirt, skimming up and over her rib cage before taking her naked breasts in his hands. His fingers pulled lightly on her nipples before soothing them in circles with his palms. She seemed to love that. Her head turned toward him, seeking his mouth for a kiss, and Derek obliged. He kissed her the way he sensed she wanted it—thorough and dirty. He licked at her until she protested, then punished her mouth for daring to ask for more.

"Derek, please. *Please*." She reached down with one hand and tried to pull off her T-shirt.

"No, no. The shirt stays on."

"Why?"

"Because if I see your naked breasts, I'm going to want to suck your pretty little nipples. And if I suck your nipples, I'm going to need to bury my cock inside you."

She moaned against his neck, her sexy ass writhing against his rampant hard-on. In that moment, he swore he'd never wanted anything more in his life than to bend Ginger forward and take what he already considered *his*.

Knowing he couldn't last much longer and still walk away, his hand slid down her stomach and slipped inside the red, silky panties she wore. Encountering her slick wetness, Derek came very close to losing his tenuous resolve. He slid his middle finger through her heat, found her swollen nub, and began his relentless assault, circling the spot in teasing strokes, driving her crazy, then rubbing and pinching where she needed it most.

Adding a second finger to increase the pressure on her clit, his eyes met hers in the mirror. They were beginning to glaze with her upcoming orgasm. His gaze dropped to where her hard nipples pressed tightly against the soaked cotton, and lower, to where his hand moved rhythmically inside her panties. It was the most arousing sight he'd ever seen. "Ginger, someday soon, I'm going to put you here in this exact position and fuck you over and over again to make up for this."

Ginger went over the edge, throwing back her head and swiveling her hips. He felt her pussy clenching and trembling against his hand, so he slid two fingers deep inside to help her ride it out. He kept his fingers moving until the spasms left her and she slumped backward against him.

Now that he'd watched Ginger come, Derek decided he could die a happy man. And if he didn't need to remove himself from her presence immediately, he would do it all over again just to re-witness her pleasure. Reluctantly, he tore his eyes away from her image in the steamed-up mirror, resting his forehead on her shoulder.

"Is this service included in the rent?" she panted.

Derek laughed into her neck, pleased as hell. Goddamn, he loved the fact that unlike most women of his experience, Ginger didn't clam up after a sexual encounter, making excuses for her behavior or questioning what it meant.

"You're not paying rent."

She sighed. "Derek."

He couldn't stop himself from running a hand over her hip, biting gently into her supple flesh with his fingers. "We'll work something else out, Ginger."

"I don't like the sound of that."

"I'm not talking about sex."

"Oh."

Derek grinned at the poorly hidden disappointment in her voice, but it quickly faded when his need ratcheted up another level. He needed to get out of there. Fast. But first, "I have a way to un-blur those lines you're so concerned about."

Involuntarily, he was sure, Ginger's eyes dropped to his mouth and he swelled larger inside his pants. "Well, let's hear it, Lieutenant."

"I need a favor."

She smirked, trying to skirt past him. "I had a feeling…"

"Not that kind of favor." He pressed a hand to her waist to keep her still and laughed under his breath. "I've been roped into attending a charity dinner tomorrow night and I need you to come with me. As my date."

Ginger didn't respond, just pinned him with a searching look.

"I told you I wouldn't accept money from you and I won't, but since you're determined to keep us on equal footing, I'd consider it payment in full for the use of the room."

"And there it is." Ginger shivered. "A date, huh? You know it's not going to be easy to find someone to cover my shift on this short of notice."

"Can you be ready by seven?"

She sighed. "Fine."

"I'll leave you to your shower while I still can."

Stifling a groan, Derek backed away from her and walked out of the bathroom.

Chapter Ten

Ginger paused in the act of spreading lotion on her arms as she heard Derek's apartment door open and close from inside the spare bedroom where she waited, fully dressed for their date.

Date. The most offensive four-letter word in the English language. It wasn't a coincidence that it rhymed with *hate*. It also rhymed with *late* and *irate*, the former of which described Derek's current *state*.

"Nice one," Ginger congratulated herself under her breath.

The wall clock told her he'd arrived exactly half an hour late to pick her up. After asking her on this date as a favor *to him*, he didn't even have the decency to show up on time. Ginger yanked off the chandelier earrings she'd put on and removed approximately eight damn times. She couldn't remember why she'd agreed to accompany him in the first place. His bartering the spare room in exchange for a date was low even by his standards. She should have called him on it and demanded he accept her money. Instead, she'd found herself agreeing, with very little persuasion on his end.

She'd spent the morning in her apartment with Lenny and the work crew he'd hired to repair the flood damage to the space. Going through her and Willa's possessions, Ginger had been relieved to find most of it, including all of their clothes, could be saved. After throwing out the damaged items, she'd taken the damp clothes to the basement laundry room and cleaned them thoroughly. Thankfully, most of her furniture projects were salvageable as well, although she'd cried while dragging the baby-themed hope chest to the curb for sanitation to pick up.

Ruined hope chest aside, they got a lot of work done in the apartment and she felt optimistic about returning home soon. Wading through her waterlogged closet, she'd pulled out the plastic garment bag containing her one and only presentable dress. *The* little black dress of her dreams. A vintage Versace she'd found at a yard sale one afternoon in Nashville after a wife unexpectedly showed up from a vacation in Saint-Tropez, found her husband's mistress living in their home, and held an impromptu sale to get rid of the younger woman's possessions.

The kicker? She'd bought it for a nickel.

Ginger stood in front of the mirror checking her appearance. To her, the silk, corseted dress symbolized everything she dreamed of being. Classy, worldly, stylish. She'd never been given a chance to wear it before, having avoided the dating scene after the Holy Trinity debacle, but sometimes put it on when she needed a pick-me-up.

She'd blown her hair dry and let it fall in waves around her shoulders, applying only a minimal amount of makeup. The women who came into Sensation usually wore heavier eyeliner and lipstick, but she always felt self-conscious with it on. Turning sideways, she flipped her hair and smiled at her reflection. Then her shoulders slumped.

She didn't know the kind of circles in which Derek moved. Maybe this dress wouldn't be considered stylish. After all, Chicago was a million miles away from Nashville in terms of how people dressed and acted. Maybe the dress really *had* only been worth a nickel.

Is it too late to cancel? I'll tell him I'm sick. Or I couldn't find anyone to cover my shift. Or maybe she should just pick a fight with him. She sure as hell knew how to accomplish that.

Ginger quickly crossed the last idea off her list. If she started an argument, they'd probably just end up making out. Or re-creating last night's scene in the bathroom.

At the reminder of last night, Ginger's pulse began pounding in her ears. Her cheeks flushed pink and she unconsciously wetted her lips. God, she'd never experienced anything like Derek touching her body. Not one of his movements had been wasted. His objective was to make her come and every motion, every flick of his fingers and kiss of his mouth, moved her toward oblivion.

Reminding herself of her earlier decision, Ginger straightened her shoulders and readied herself to face Derek in the kitchen. Clearly, he desired a physical relationship with her. And she with him. They were both consenting, single adults. And damn, he excited the hell out of her. The things he said. The liberties he took. The way he seemed attuned to her body and needs.

She could keep it physical, Ginger assured herself. She could control how it proceeded. How it ended. Because it *would* end. Ginger didn't know the first thing about a functional relationship.

When she was thirteen, her mother brought home a line cook from the local barbecue joint named Seth. He hung around for about three months, the longest a man had ever stayed in their home. There was talk at the breakfast table about marriage. Weddings. Adopting her and Willa. Then one day, Seth never came back. Her mother didn't leave her bedroom for a week and when she did, she parked herself on the couch and chain-smoked between sips of scotch for over a month while Ginger begged the neighbors for food scraps to feed Willa.

Granted, she considered herself a stronger woman than Valerie. But with her past, combined with the sob stories she heard nightly behind the bar, Ginger steered clear of any messy entanglements.

Only a few minutes had passed when she heard Derek exit his bedroom and enter the kitchen. Figures, it only took him five minutes to get ready when it took her a full hour. After taking one final, soothing breath, Ginger stepped into her black pumps, picked up her clutch purse, and left the bedroom.

Derek stood at the refrigerator gulping down a bottle of water, the white dress shirt stretched across his broad shoulders. At the click of her shoes against the hardwood floor, he turned to look at her.

And stopped cold.

Ginger panicked, unable to judge from his expression whether he approved of her attire or not. He looked utterly perfect in his tuxedo. Sophisticated. Someone accustomed to big-city standards. He wore the garment like a second skin, every movement masculine and fluid. The five o'clock shadow darkening his jaw and the lack of sleep evident on his face saved him from being completely intimidating, but she couldn't help a shiver of apprehension upon seeing him dressed this way. He looked ready to command a room. Or her. Goose bumps broke out along her arms.

Damned if she was going to let him know how he affected her.

Placing a hand on her hip, Ginger tossed her hair over her shoulder and stood her ground, letting him look his fill. And he did. Sharp, green eyes tracked upward from her thighs, over her hips to her breasts.

He crooked a finger at her. "Come here." His voice sounded raw and uneven.

Refusing to be intimidated, Ginger crossed the living room to where Derek stood unmoving in the kitchen. She could swear his eyes darkened as she got closer.

"You're late."

"And you're fucking gorgeous."

Her breath caught in her throat. Tearing her eyes away from his voracious gaze, she set her shawl and clutch down on the counter. "Thank you, Lieutenant. You look nice, too. Doesn't excuse the fact that you're late."

"I'm sorry. You should never have to wait for anyone." Derek came up behind where she'd leaned a hip against the counter. His breath feathered over her bare shoulder, moving a few strands of her hair against her neck. "What color are your panties?"

"Excuse me?" Her voice sounded thin to her own ears.

"You heard me."

She swallowed the knot in her throat. "Why?"

"Baby, if I'm going to take you into a room full of men wearing that dress, I'm damn well going to be the only one who knows the color of your panties."

A rush of liquid heat moved through her, settling between her legs. His voice alone could do that to her. The deep, thick quality of it stroked over her body the way she now knew his hands would. Part of Ginger wanted to continue chastising him for his lateness to dissipate the lust clouding the air around them. The rest of her yearned for whatever he had planned for her.

He stood so incredibly close without touching her. Even so, she felt like his hands were moving all over her body. His proximity combined with his coffee-and-leather scent made her flesh tingle. Her breathing accelerated with every second that passed and he still didn't touch her.

"Not going to answer? Okay." Finally, his skin made contact with hers and Ginger's breath shuddered out. They stood flush, his front to her back, his breath warming the skin of her neck. "Place your hands flat on the counter."

What? Why won't he just kiss me? Confused by his request, she remained mostly still save the breaths causing her chest to rise and fall rapidly. Her breasts swelled against the top of her dress with each panting breath, begging for Derek's hands to touch them.

"Do as you're told."

Ginger's arousal outweighed the flicker of annoyance brought on by Derek's command, so she gently placed her palms facedown on the cold surface of the kitchen counter, leaving her slightly bent over at the waist. Unable to see Derek, she could only sense him moving behind her.

Suddenly, her feet were kicked wider by Derek's dress shoe, and the already-exposed position she stood in became twice as vulnerable. Ginger made a surprised sound at his roughness, but forced herself to remain the way he'd posed her. She tried to imagine what Derek saw from behind, bent over the counter as she stood with her legs spread shoulder-width apart. She could hear his harsh breathing and imagined him sizing her up. Deciding what to do next. The anticipation dried her mouth.

His hands moved up the sides of her thighs to the hem of her dress, massaging as they went. Then he lifted her skirt, sliding the silky material up the tops of her legs and over her ass. He made a strangled sound, then a long stretch of silence passed, the only sound in the room their heavy breathing.

"No panties, Ginger?"

She closed her eyes, savoring the tortured quality to his voice. "I can't wear any with this dress. The outline would be noticeable."

"I see."

Derek's hand came down hard on her exposed backside, jarring her stomach against the edge of the counter. The slap of his large palm against her bare flesh echoed through the room.

"Oh!"

Shocked by the sudden sting, it took Ginger a few seconds to realize he'd spanked her. She wasn't given time to think any further because he did it again. And again. He spanked her five times, each time harder than the last until her bottom smarted painfully.

Despite the burn each slap earned her, Ginger couldn't help wishing him to continue, despite her warring emotions. His punishing slaps heightened her senses, making her aware of every breath leaving her lungs, every groan escaping Derek's throat. Warmth pooled low in her belly and spread to her legs until they felt like jelly. Her thighs shook with the need to press together, but his foot, inserted firmly between her high heels, prevented it. She was unnerved by her reaction. She was excited by it.

The fifth time Derek's palm connected with her flesh, she found herself pushing higher on her toes, presenting herself to him. Asking for it. Sensations and emotions clouded her brain. She tried to straighten, to make sense of the heat coiling low in her belly, but he placed a hand firmly on her back, keeping her bent over the counter.

"You like that, beautiful girl?" When she whimpered, he leaned over and spoke directly into her ear. "Good. That was for the hard-on I'll be walking around with tonight. And you'll goddamn wear the imprint of my hand on your ass for it."

His arrogant statement brought Ginger out of her momentary state of shock. She pushed away from the counter, forcing him off of her. The blatant hunger on his face gave her pause. His cheekbones were flushed red, his fists clenched at his sides as if he struggled not to reach for her.

"If you bend over, even slightly, in that dress while we're out tonight, I will spank your beautiful ass again in front of everyone present. Do you understand me, Ginger?"

She yanked the dress back into place over her still-stinging backside. "Go ahead. It still wouldn't be the worst date I ever had."

His eyes narrowed dangerously. "Don't test me on this. I'm already less than thrilled about bringing you out in public looking like that."

"Like what?"

"Like a walking wet dream."

Her mouth opened and closed. To hide her shock, she turned and snatched her clutch and shawl off the counter. "I'm not changing, so deal with it."

"I just did."

"You're an arrogant jackass, you know that?"

He nodded. "Let's go. We're running late thanks to you."

Chapter Eleven

Derek took Ginger's shawl and handed it to the coat-check attendant, grimacing when the black dress revealed itself once more. It was going to be one bitch of a long night.

The black, silky material displayed every curve and nuance of her body to perfection, exposing just the right amount of cleavage to keep a man watching and begging for her to lean forward a little too far. Her skin glowed against the dark material of the dress, making his hands itch to touch.

How could he have been so close earlier and not tasted her?

An irritated sound drew his attention back to Ginger's stunning face to reveal those plump lips pressed together in displeasure. "I don't care if I'm wearing four-inch heels, I will walk home if you're determined to frown at me all night, Derek."

God, she'd just had to remind him of the damn shoes. Each of her legs looked a mile long in them. He wanted to rip off the dress and wrap those legs around his waist.

He needed to get a hold of himself. The fact that she'd still agreed to come with him tonight after his earlier behavior blew his mind. He'd spanked her. *Hard*. Something he'd wanted to do since that night on the roof, but never dreamed he'd act on. In every one of his fantasies about Ginger, permission was never required, but this hadn't been a fantasy and he'd acted on impulse. Seeing her walk out in that dress nearly brought him to his knees, but her lack of panties had pushed him hurtling over the edge.

For as long as Derek lived, he would never forget the vision of Ginger bent over his kitchen counter to receive her spanking. She'd been the perfect combination of defiant and vulnerable. He could still hear the slap of his hand against her bare flesh ringing in his head.

Every day, the need within him grew greater, more painful. His actions tonight proved just how little restraint he had left. The fact that she didn't reprimand him for his actions, and in fact *enjoyed,* if not craved his ministrations, only made him want to push her further.

Even now, as the young coat-check attendant's eyes roamed over Ginger, Derek had to resist the compulsion to haul her over his shoulder and take her home.

Which certainly wouldn't earn him any points with the woman in question.

Get your shit together, Tyler.

He composed his features and offered Ginger his arm. "Come on. Let's see if we can hunt you up some of that cheap red wine you're so fond of."

"Oh no, Lieutenant. Tonight I'm drinking the good stuff."

Derek led Ginger through the gilded double doors leading into the banquet hall, and immediately spotted a group of homicide detectives from his station. Wanting to avoid that mess for as long as possible, he steered Ginger in the opposite direction, toward the bar, where he ordered her a glass of wine and a whiskey for himself. Since he'd be driving, he'd only allow himself the one drink. If he was spending the evening with Ginger, he'd damn well need it.

Soft music drifted through the room. Big band combined with the healthy dose of Sinatra required at all political events. One end of the room held a candlelit dining area with thirty-odd tables, a stage, and a podium located toward the front. A currently half-empty dance floor took up the other half of the room. Uniformed servers in black and white rushed through the packed cocktail and dining area offering champagne flutes and hors d'oeuvres to guests.

Derek spotted the mayor and several prominent councilmen rubbing elbows with local law enforcement and shook his head, wondering how many of them were on one another's payroll. Since making lieutenant two years ago, he'd been approached several times and propositioned about dropping charges for a friend of a friend, or looking the other way when the governor's son was present at the scene of a crime, but Derek refused to compromise himself to retain his position. Small favors often turned into full-time obligations, and he had no ambitions of being a political lackey.

He looked down at Ginger, who sipped her wine and observed the room through wide eyes. It felt wrong, bringing her to this place where criminals posed as saviors to the city. Although she'd undoubtedly come across her share of unsavory characters in her past, here they posed as something else entirely. Once again, Derek tamped down the need to whisk her home, away from this place. Where he could have her to himself.

"We don't have to stay all night, you know. An hour should do it."

Ginger looked surprised, her wineglass pausing halfway to her lips. "We just got here."

Her expression turned unsure, as if worried she might be the reason he wanted to leave. He hurried to clarify. "These events are exhausting. Too much grinning and bullshitting."

Her face spread into a slow smile. "Well, you're in luck, sweetheart. I grin and bullshit for a living."

Derek sipped his whiskey. "These aren't the type of men who frequent Sensation."

"Maybe not now, but they all were at one time or another." Something over his shoulder caught her attention. "And I'm fairly certain this group of gentlemen headed our way came to see me in Sensation just this week."

Inwardly wincing, Derek turned to see Barker, Alvarez, and two other detectives heading in their direction. Taking a step closer to Ginger, he nodded in acknowledgment.

"Lieutenant Tyler," Alvarez greeted him, raising an approving eyebrow at Ginger. Alvarez had been a detective long before Derek joined the force and tended to get away with more than the other men due to seniority. There'd been a few months of tension when the higher-ups passed him over for the lieutenant position in favor of Derek, but it eventually passed and Derek considered him his best detective.

"Alvarez."

He leaned past Derek to address Ginger. "I don't think we've formally met, but I recall you make one hell of a vodka gimlet."

She flashed him a blinding smile. "I'm Ginger. Next time, I'll make you one of my famous mojitos if you promise not to scare off the rest of my customers."

The other three men looked uncomfortably at Derek, but Alvarez just laughed. "Just following up on a hot tip that Sensation is where all the cool kids hang out. Besides, I can't help how someone interprets my looks."

"That sounds like typical cop logic."

Alvarez tried to get around Derek to continue his conversation with Ginger, but stopped when he saw his lieutenant's expression. "And I'm interpreting the boss's look to say *back off.*"

If Derek didn't know for a fact that Alvarez was happily married with two children, he would have passed on the message sooner. However, he didn't know the marital status of the other three men, nor did he care. Ginger belonged to *him.*

She nudged him with her elbow, a subtle reminder of her earlier threat to walk home. "Mr. Alvarez, maybe you can tell me what this event is being held for. Derek hasn't had time to tell me yet."

Alvarez sent Derek a look of censure, which he ignored. Pulling Barker forward, Alvarez explained. "This gentleman who hasn't said two words since we came over here, and I can't *imagine* why, is Councilman Barker's nephew. We're all here on his uncle's dime. Normally, Lieutenant Tyler is the only one required to play dress-up and kiss politician ass. Thanks to Barker, we all have to pucker up tonight."

Ginger laughed, reaching forward to shake Barker's hand. Derek gave a mental eye roll when Barker's eyes practically glazed over at the contact. "And tonight's cause, Mr. Barker?"

The rookie puffed up a little. "My uncle is leading a committee to organize after-school programs in the city's worst neighborhoods. To help keep local kids from joining gangs and get into sports or academic pursuits instead."

"Damn, Barker. Did you rehearse that in the mirror?" Alvarez joked, signaling the bartender.

Barker flushed. "Anyway, you'll hear more about it at dinner, Ginger."

She smiled broadly at him. "I look forward to it."

Derek had seen quite enough of Ginger smiling at other men for one evening. He couldn't recall her ever smiling at him like that. Sliding an arm around her bare shoulders, he excused them and led her toward their assigned seats.

Already seated at the round, ten-person table was Patty, the dispatch operator responsible for his bringing Ginger in the first place. Also waiting for dinner to start was Kenny, his ex-partner, and Lisa, Derek's ex-girlfriend, still an item apparently. Thankfully, they were across the table, blocked by an obscenely large centerpiece, saving him from having to make introductions.

Patty, however, stood to greet him with a kiss on the cheek. "Derek, you brought a date!"

Wanting to roll his eyes at Patty's false shock, Derek placed a hand on Ginger's back and guided her forward. "Ginger, this is Patty. She works dispatch and is *unfortunately* leaving us soon to terrorize her husband full-time."

The older woman laughed in delight, and Derek couldn't help but grin in response. Despite being her favorite target for practical jokes, he liked Patty quite a lot and would be sad to see her go.

"Oh, Lieutenant. You know you're going to miss me like hell."

"I think I might, Patty."

Trying to hide her pleasure over his words, she turned to Ginger with a sly smile. "And how do you know this asshole, honey?"

Ginger nearly choked on her wine. "Oh, um, Derek and I are roommates."

Her eyebrows shot up. "Roommates? Aren't you a little old for a roommate, Derek?"

Ginger answered before he could. "It's only temporary, actually. My apartment across the hall, where I live with my sister, flooded last night. Derek insisted we take his spare room. He was very heroic, actually."

Patty snorted. "I'm sure it's been a real hardship for him. But since you're only roommates, maybe I can set Ginger up with my single nephew. He lives right here in Chicago."

"I take it back, Patty," Derek grumbled. "You can retire with my blessing."

A man in a tuxedo approached the microphone and asked for the guests to take their seats. Derek held the chair next to Patty out for Ginger, then took the seat on the opposite side. Alvarez and a few other detectives joined them a minute later.

Dinner went smoothly, Ginger and Patty chatting happily while his and Alvarez's discussion inevitably turned to work. His informant continued to balk about Modesto's whereabouts, but Alvarez thought he'd found some leverage he could use.

His eyes continually met Ginger's even though they didn't speak during the meal. She'd quickly earned Patty's admiration, and by the time dessert was brought out, Ginger had been inundated with pictures and stories about the woman's grandson, which she smiled and cooed over dutifully. Derek marveled over how well she fit in among his peers. He usually found himself checking his watch obsessively during these functions, but watching Ginger giggle charmingly and sip wine made time move too quickly. He hadn't expected tonight to feel so natural, even if he'd been forced to glare at a few passing suits ogling his date during the second course.

"Damn, Lieutenant. Do I have to put on a black dress and heels to keep your attention tonight?"

Derek dragged his eyes away from Ginger and turned back to Alvarez with a smirk. "I don't think it comes in your size."

"Ouch. I can't help that I got a woman at home who can cook."

"I hope you leave enough for the kids to eat."

"Oh, he's got jokes, does he? This girl is good for you, Lieutenant. I knew you had a sense of humor in there somewhere."

The tuxedoed man approached the microphone once more, calling for the room's attention. Conversation slowly came to a halt around them. "Ladies and gentlemen, I have the honor of bringing Councilman Barker to the stage. His charity, Chicago Takes the Lead, is the reason we are all here this evening. So without further ado, please welcome Councilman Leon Barker."

As the audience clapped politely, the councilman, a distinguished-looking man in his early fifties, took the stage. A spotlight found him as he approached the podium, highlighting the silver streaks in his black hair. He surveyed the room winningly, like a man used to making speeches, and smiled his thanks for their applause. "Thank you for coming. I hope you'll all remember how great that prime rib was come election time."

The politicians laughed in response. "As you are aware, we began Chicago Takes the Lead thirteen years ago and have implemented several after-school programs throughout the inner city of Chicago, mainly in the district I'm honored to represent. What makes Chicago Takes the Lead unique is our boys in blue. In addition to teachers and social workers, Chicago's finest have been kind enough to volunteer their time to become mentors to our youth. We couldn't do it without them."

When the applause died down once more, he went on to describe the inner workings of the charity and its day-to-day operations. He didn't mention the fact that many of the youths they mentored went on to take the police department entrance exam, making the charity a glorified recruiting operation targeting inner-city children. Not only did it assist Chicago in strengthening police ranks year by year, but it also facilitated the early establishment of relationships between politicians and the police force—both facets of the system that didn't sit well with Derek, and a sentiment he'd been sure to share with the councilman whenever he received an invitation to speak at a Takes the Lead event.

The lights dimmed and a slide show began, showing snapshots of youths playing soccer alongside local law enforcement or painting over graffiti in downtown Chicago. A series of shots depicted a Thanksgiving meal, catered by the councilman's office no doubt, being served in a school gymnasium.

Glancing over to gauge Ginger's reaction, he started in his seat at tears welling in her eyes. All at once the reason for her distress became apparent. Jesus. How could he have brought her here?

Chapter Twelve

Derek's hand grasped her cold fingers under the table, startling her. Hand-holding didn't seem like a typical Derek move and she reacted warily. But the warmth his much bigger hand offered felt good and right, so she slid her hand into his and squeezed. He squeezed back.

She shouldn't be crying. If anyone saw her welling up over this puffed-up public service announcement, it would embarrass the hell out of her. And Derek, too.

Blinking furiously, Ginger tried to disengage herself from the images flashing across the screen. Hungry children thankfully receiving a turkey leg and some stuffing. A young girl smiling as someone handed her a shiny pink winter coat at a local coat drive. It brought back painful images of sending Willa out to school in thirty-degree weather wearing a threadbare sweatshirt. Or sharing a can of stolen pumpkin pie filling on Thanksgiving Day. These were things she tried not to think about anymore, but avoiding the past now proved impossible as images continued to play under a cheerful voiceover.

The evening had been going so well until now. Good wine, amazing food, friendly people. She'd truly been enjoying herself. Even Derek appeared to get over his initial annoyance over her attire and had started smiling at her. Derek in a tuxedo was a breathtaking sight. Throw in a smile on top of that and you had one dangerously irresistible man. His scent teased her, reminding her constantly how close he sat, how little she'd have to move to be touching him. Sitting in his lap.

Then the slideshow started and everything ceased to exist around her. The past blurred everything out, threatening to expose her as an imposter in this room full of rich people.

When the lights came on, Ginger let go of Derek's hand and pretended to dig in her clutch so no one would notice her puffy eyes. He suddenly stood behind her, pulling her chair back.

"Come on. Dance with me."

Grateful for the chance to escape their table, Ginger didn't dwell on her surprise over Derek's invitation. Standing, she took his hand once more and let him lead her out onto the floor where several other couples danced to a soft instrumental. Finding an open spot, he pulled her into his arms.

A sigh escaped Ginger before she could stop it. Her body fit perfectly against his in her heels, bringing her head just under his chin. The expensive aftershave scent emanating from his throat smelled near enough to taste. They'd never stood this close to each other before without something sexual transpiring between them, and the reality of that pulsed in the air like a living, breathing thing.

To distract herself from those memories, she counted his flaws. Stubble appeared on his jaw much too quickly after shaving. His dark hair was cut too short, giving a woman nothing to sink her fingers into if the mood struck her.

Aw hell, who was she kidding? The man kicked her libido into warp speed just by existing. As they swayed to the music, he held on to her tightly, one hand riding just above her ass, sending a message to every other man in the room that he'd be the only one seeing her naked tonight. It infuriated her. It turned her on so crazily, she could hardly focus on the dance.

"I'm sorry."

She tipped her head back to meet his eyes. "What are you sorry about?"

His gaze penetrated hers. "You were upset during the slideshow. I'm sorry."

Ginger attempted a smile to disguise the painful drumming of her heart, but didn't think she succeeded. She wished Derek hadn't reminded her. "You don't have anything to apologize for. I guess I was just thinking about someone who could have used a program like this back in Nashville." She paused. "Even if it is just a recruitment program in disguise."

Derek's face registered surprise. "Picked up on that, did you?"

She shrugged, casting a glance over at their table where several detectives were still seated. "You seem so young to be their lieutenant. How did that happen?"

Apart from his shoulders tensing underneath her hands, his demeanor stayed the same. "It's not a very pleasant story."

"Okay. You don't have to tell me."

The hand riding just below her waist pulled her even closer. "New Year's Eve three years ago, there was a hostage situation involving a Lithuanian man who'd been fired as a messenger from some major company located downtown in the Old Colony Building. I'd just made detective, and my partner at the time, Kenny, spoke fluent Lithuanian. His parents are first-generation immigrants and he happens to be the only man in the department with that particular skill."

His hand skimmed up her back, moving underneath her hair, where he began stroking her neck gently. Ginger struggled to focus on his soothingly deep voice as he continued the story.

"Kenny translated for the hostage negotiator and they seemed to be getting through to him, calming him down. Then one of the hostages tried to escape and was shot and killed for his efforts. The whole operation went to hell, the perp aware that his new status as murderer wouldn't buy him any demands. They were getting ready to send in a SWAT team, but because of the building's layout, he would probably have seen it coming and shot more people before they could stop him."

She sensed him nearing the uncomfortable part of the story. "The Old Colony Building is a landmark and I'd studied it in college during an architecture course. I knew a different way into the building that would bring us onto the same floor without alerting him to our presence. They didn't like putting their faith in a brand-new detective, but I led a team inside, through the back of the building, and took the perp down through a vent in the ceiling."

"Sounds like you paid attention in class." Ginger leaned back, studying his frown. "That's a great story, save the one unfortunate death. It could have been a lot worse."

"You asked me how I made lieutenant." He glanced away. "One of the hostages turned out to be the mayor's granddaughter. When he got wind of my role in the takedown, he demanded the department promote me. I didn't earn it. They handed it to me."

Ginger scoffed in disbelief, but his expression remained tight so she leaned in and spoke quietly against his shoulder. "Derek, people have gotten ahead in this world for much less. A lot of them are probably in this room right now."

He leaned down to rest his mouth against her temple.

"You're right about that."

She shivered. In order to kiss him, she needed only tip her head back and meet his lips. But they stood in the middle of a crowded dance floor filled with his peers, so she appeased herself by pressing closer to his warm chest. His arm tightened around her, the hand in her hair tugging lightly on the strands.

"So being a lieutenant isn't all about fancy charity events like this one. There's a lot of danger involved."

He nodded against her head but didn't respond.

Ginger could sense the direction of his thoughts. "I wish I'd known that day in the hallway you were headed to a funeral. I still feel a little guilty about telling you to go to hell."

"If I recall correctly, I deserved it."

She wrinkled her nose, then sighed. "Well, it certainly isn't an easy life you've chosen for yourself. I'm sorry I added to it that particular day. Even if you *did* deserve it."

The hand in her hair began massaging her neck. "It hasn't been easy for you, either. Has it?"

Ginger didn't show any reaction to his casually posed question, but her internal defenses shot to attention. "That's a story for a different day."

She sensed him wanting to press her for more, but he wisely refrained. A heavy silence descended between them as they danced, and Ginger searched her brain for a way to lighten the mood again.

"Patty mentioned something interesting during dinner."

"Did she?"

"Hmm. She took some liberties in responding to your invitation tonight."

His chest rumbled with laughter against her cheek. "So it *was* her. I had a feeling."

Reluctantly, Ginger pulled away to look up into his face.

Being held by him felt too natural, like she could crawl into his arms and fall asleep. But cuddling and neck massages were not a part of what they were doing here together, and she needed to remind herself of that fact. Derek was the same man who spanked her without warning, pleasured her in front of a mirror so he could watch. She shouldn't feel safe with him, but she did. It forced her to question her judgment.

The first Derek, the one who breathed sensuality, whose very words elicited a response from her body, *that* Derek she could accept. Warm, humble, apologetic Derek quite frankly terrified her.

Someone needed to redraw the battle lines, and it looked like it would be up to her.

She gazed up at him through her lashes. "Surely, Lieutenant, you keep a few women on reserve to bring to events like this, or maybe just the occasional late-night date. Why not call one of them? You and I want something from each other and it doesn't include prime rib dinners and dancing."

His eyes narrowed suspiciously and Ginger sensed he could see right through her. "You told me to try harder. I'm just following orders."

"I didn't think you were in any condition to pay attention that night."

"I always pay attention where you're concerned."

The song ended and after a moment, Derek let his arms drop, shoving his hands into his pants pockets. People around them made their way to the bar or returned to their tables, but Derek and Ginger remained rooted in place.

"Since you appear to be the expert, what do we want from each other, Ginger?"

"I think you know."

"Oh, I do. But I want to hear you say it."

Painfully aware of the crowd milling around them, she

stepped closer and reached up to adjust his bow tie, lowering her voice to a near-whisper. "I want to show you instead."

Derek's quick exhalation of breath stirred the hair on her head. His hand banded around her elbow, steering her off the dance floor. "We're leaving. Now."

Startled by his reaction, Ginger stopped him before they reached the table. "Wait. I need to use the ladies' room. I'll meet you at the coat check."

He looked like he wanted to argue, so she turned and slipped through the crowd toward the restroom before he could grab her again. Thankfully she didn't have to wait in line and the opulent bathroom was relatively empty, save the uniformed attendant handing out paper towels and breath mints.

Washing her hands and giving herself a quick glance in the mirror, Ginger turned to leave but stopped abruptly when a tall blonde entered the bathroom. She recognized the woman from their table, but hadn't been introduced, nor were they given an opportunity to speak during dinner. Easily six inches taller than Ginger, she looked elegant in a pale gray cocktail dress, which highlighted the icy blue of her eyes.

"Well hello there," the blonde slurred, leaning a little too close to her. Ginger smiled back indulgently, having spent the better part of her life associating with drunken people. It required walking a fine line between friendly and patronizing. She liked to think her technique had been perfected.

"Hi. I recognize you from my table. We didn't get a chance to meet, though. I'm Ginger." She held out her hand, but the woman simply looked at it and laughed hysterically.

"Oh, my God. Please say that accent isn't real."

"Real, I'm afraid." *Unlike your breasts.* "Guess you don't hear many Tennessee accents in Chicago."

"Nope." She pretended to look thoughtful. "I guess it must be kind of a novelty for someone like Derek. Although I'm surprised he'd bring you to such an important event sounding like...I don't know, a cowgirl or something." Apparently, she found that awfully funny and sunk against the wall in a fit of laughter.

Ginger somehow kept the smile glued to her face. "I'm sorry, I didn't catch your name."

"I'm Lisa."

She stepped around the other woman, intent on exiting the bathroom. "Well, Lisa, it's been lovely. But I can't just spend all night in the bathroom."

"I know exactly what you'll be spending the night doing, cowgirl."

Ginger sighed and pushed away from the door. "Listen up, sweetheart. For all your outrageous subtlety, it's obvious you have a problem with me. Care to share?"

"It's not so much a problem. More of an explanation."

The obvious agenda on the blonde's face sent a warning shiver up Ginger's spine, but she ignored it. "Don't let me stop you."

Lisa smirked. "You see, I'm here with Kenny, Derek's ex-partner. We've been together about two years, but before that it was me and Derek."

Ginger schooled her features, not wanting to give Lisa the reaction she desired, but ice formed in the pit of her stomach. "Is that all?"

"Honey, you must be wondering why Derek brought you here. At first, I was a little confused, too. You're hardly his type." She swayed a little in her laughter then refocused squarely on Ginger. "I left Derek for Kenny. He's never gotten over it. You're simply here to piss me off."

Ginger tilted her head sadly. "Looks like it worked."

"Oh, fuck you, Bessie." In her drunken state, the woman tilted to the left and nearly sprawled on her ass, but Ginger caught her arm at the last moment. Lashing out with a growl of rage, she pushed Ginger away. "I just wanted him to see what he'd be missing," she spat, red-faced. "I didn't think he'd leave for good."

Time to go. Ginger beelined toward the door, but somehow Lisa moved quickly enough to stop her once more. "Have you fucked him yet? I know you have. I saw the way he looked at you. Enjoy it while it lasts, cowgirl. You'll never get it that good again."

Chapter Thirteen

With the reluctant bathroom attendant's help, Ginger finally managed to get past Lisa and out of the bathroom. She pushed through the swinging door and nearly ran into Derek waiting for her on the other side, holding her shawl. One look at his face and she knew he'd seen Lisa enter the bathroom behind her.

Ginger stormed past him, through the lively banquet hall and lobby, encountering a few curious looks as she passed. She found herself on the dark street outside the hotel before she took a single breath. Derek's hand wrapped around her arm, stopping her before she could hail a cab.

"Slow down. What the hell happened in there?" She spun on Derek and his irritated expression vanished. "Talk to me," he implored.

"I've just been accosted by your hammered ex-girlfriend in the bathroom."

"Jesus." He pinched the bridge of his nose. "What did she say to you?"

Ginger ignored the question. "You know what I don't

understand, Derek? Why you weren't just honest with me. We're not dating. We barely *like* each other. You told me this date was a favor *to you*. If you'd explained your reasons for bringing me along, we could have put on a *real* good show for old Lisa. Hell, if you'd asked nicely, I might have let you feel me up on the dance floor."

He stared at her for a minute, expression confused, then took her arm and led her down the sidewalk, away from the hotel. A valet attendant even jumped out of his way to let them pass. *Nice.*

"Let me *go*."

"No."

Upon arriving, Derek had parked his SUV down an empty side street adjacent to the hotel, placing a police department placard in the windshield so it wouldn't be towed. In the night's darkness, the street now resembled more of an alley, steam rising in white curls from manhole covers and zero traffic passing by.

Having no choice but to trip after him in her heels, she fumed in silence at Derek's back the entire way to the car. Reaching it, he whirled around to face her.

"Are you jealous?"

Sputtering, she pulled her arm out of his grasp. "*Excuse me?*"

"You are." He nodded slowly. "Good."

"You have no idea how close you are to a painful death right now."

Derek stepped closer and Ginger held up a hand to stop him. He merely kept coming, pressing his chest against her palm and groaning at the simple contact.

"I don't play bullshit mind games, Ginger. I brought you here for a lot of reasons. Making Lisa jealous definitely wasn't one of them."

Ginger scrutinized Derek's face closely to judge his

sincerity and sensed him telling the truth. He'd been upfront with her since the beginning of their association about what he wanted. Mind games simply weren't his style. If she allowed herself to be honest, she'd hardly believed Lisa in the first place.

So why didn't she feel reassured? His words did nothing to soothe the foreign emotions swirling around, bumping into each other inside her chest. She felt out of control, a little giddy. She wanted to slap Derek across the face just so he'd chase her down and make her pay for it. None of her thoughts made sense.

Derek had been watching her carefully. Now he stepped closer, right into her space. Ginger's back came up against the SUV. Tipping her face up using her chin, Derek's eyes narrowed thoughtfully on her face.

"Unbelievable. You're still jealous, aren't you?"

Her voice shook. "Let go of me. Get away from me."

"No. I want you to explain. Explain to me why."

She glared up at him.

He leaned down and his breath feathered across her forehead, then down to her ear where he spoke in a coaxing voice. "I can *make* you talk, baby. Is that what you want? If you need my hand between your legs, all you have to do is ask me."

Before Ginger could form the words to protest, Derek's hand slid up her inner thigh and under the skirt of her dress to cup her intimately. Ginger's head fell back against the car window and she moaned without shame. The anxious feeling in her stomach fled, replaced with sharp longing.

How had he known exactly what she needed? She hadn't even known herself. All night, she'd felt achy and off-kilter. Was this the reason? She'd craved his touch this badly?

Derek's voice rasped against her neck. "Is that better? I shouldn't have spanked you earlier when we didn't have time for more. You've needed me inside you."

His thumb slipped through her folds and grazed her clitoris. Ginger cried out, but anticipating her reaction, Derek swallowed the sound with his own mouth, holding her up with his body.

He spoke against her mouth, provoking her. "Did you like being spanked, beautiful girl? Would you like me to do it harder next time?"

His questions re-created images of the earlier punishment. Every time she'd sat down throughout the evening, she'd been reminded of it. And the reason for it.

That was for the hard-on I'll be walking around with tonight.

"Yes, but you already knew that." Her words ended in a shaky breath as he slipped two fingers inside her.

"Good, I like it when you're honest with me. Now tell me why you're jealous."

Her thighs quaked on either side of his hand, showing him without words how badly she needed him to continue his expert torture. Panting breaths, *hers*, filled the silence following his command. She looked into his eyes, staggered by the intensity there.

"*Tell me*," Derek growled, placing his lips flush against hers, but not kissing her. "I want to taste your jealousy."

To hell with it. The words rushed out against his mouth before she could stop them. "Yes! I'm jealous, you asshole! I don't like her knowing what it's like to fuck you when I don't. I hate it. *I hate it!*"

Before the words were completely free of her mouth, Derek threw open the passenger side door, scooped her up in his arms, and deposited her on the leather seat, slamming the door behind her. Then he rounded the front of the car, watching her all the while through the windshield. She barely had time to register shock over what she'd said out loud before

Derek climbed in the car and started the engine.

The only sound in the car was the hum of the motor for several moments before he spoke.

"Listen to me, baby. From the time we walk in the door to my apartment, you will have less than a minute before I put my cock inside you. No foreplay. No kissing. There won't be any time, because you've got me strung so damn tight I can barely think straight. I need you to keep yourself wet for me on the ride home. Starting now." Reaching across the car's console, he yanked her skirt high on her thighs. "Put your hand between your legs, Ginger."

Reeling from his bold declaration, it took a moment for Derek's request to penetrate. He couldn't be serious. Touch herself in the car? "What if someone sees me?"

"There's no way I'd let that happen."

Throwing the car in gear, Derek issued a terse command for her to buckle her seat belt, then peeled away from the curb. They reached a red light at the corner and she still hadn't moved to obey Derek's earlier order. His eyes moved over her, scorching everything in their path, prompting Ginger to look down at herself, curious over what he saw. Her breasts, puffy with arousal, strained against the top of her dress, practically spilling out. Bare legs stretched all the way up to her naked lap, which he'd exposed by hiking up her dress.

His breathing roughened from across the car, and all at once, his reaction filled her with confidence and weakened her inhibitions. Suddenly, the soft leather beneath her ass felt glorious. The car's oversize seat made her feel delicate, feminine, sexy. Knowing how closely Derek watched, her hips moved, tested the feeling of leather against her nakedness. Her thighs pressed together. Slid apart.

Ginger's eyelids dropped, her head tipped back. She pictured Derek, how he'd looked last night. Shirtless and damp, his arm muscles shifting and bulging as he pleasured her with his hand.

Of its own volition, one hand moved to her thigh, caressing the inside with soft fingertips. Derek made a rough sound in the darkness. The stoplight must have turned green because he cursed, punching the gas to fly through the intersection.

The vibration of the car engine caused the leather to shake against her naked core. Gasping at the sensation, Ginger's hand glided higher, finally slipping between her legs.

"Good girl. Show me how you touch yourself."

His voice sounded like gravel and stroked over her like a rough caress. She wanted to replace her hand with his bigger, more skillful one, and told him so out loud.

"*God,* baby. Me, too. Just a little bit longer."

Using two fingers, Ginger found the place needing the most attention and stroked over it gently at first, moaning at the delicious pressure, then faster until her hips moved restlessly on the seat, begging for release.

"Don't you dare come, Ginger. Not yet. You'll come with me inside you tonight or not at all."

She barely heard him. Release was only seconds away. She could feel the tightening of her muscles, the trembling beginning in her upper thighs and moving higher. Derek's scent surrounded her in his car, pushing her even closer to the edge.

Suddenly, her hand was gone from between her thighs and being held in Derek's shaking grip.

"*Enough.*"

Ginger tried to pull her hand free, her breath shuddering in and out. She started to call him every filthy name in the book, but the words died on her lips when she perceived the raw agony on his face. Jaw clenched tight, eyes bright and glazed. His harsh breaths matched hers, echoing through the car's interior.

Her hooded eyes dropped to his lap, widening at the

thick erection pressed against his dress pants. The sight of his arousal made her pulse kick even higher. She reached for him, but his grip on her wrist tightened almost painfully.

"No. If you touch me there, we won't make it. I'll have to pull over and fuck you on the hood of the car."

Ginger nearly begged him to do it. As out of control as she felt, roadside sex seemed perfectly reasonable.

The light changed and Derek burned rubber through another intersection, taking a left turn onto their street once he reached the end of the block. Their building came into view on the right.

He pulled into a parking space behind the structure, threw the car in park, and rounded the car before she'd even removed her seat belt. Ginger's door was flung open. Brusquely, Derek reached in the car to adjust her dress until she once again appeared decent, then grasped her around the waist and pulled her out with little effort. Her heels clicked as she landed on the concrete.

He placed a firm hand on her back, propelling her toward the building. "Walk."

"Derek, wait."

He tensed, but didn't stop walking. They'd reached the second floor and stood just outside his apartment door before she found her voice. "She can't hear us. My sister. Please, Derek."

His hand froze in the act of unlocking the door before it resumed turning the key. With a curt nod of acknowledgment, he pushed the door open and scooped her in his arms.

"What are you doing?" she whispered. "I can walk."

"Your heels will make too much noise on the wood floor."

"Oh. Why don't I just take them off?"

"I want them on."

Ginger felt a delicious tightening in her stomach and she clung tighter to his shoulders. He marched them through the dark apartment and into his bedroom, then kicked the door shut behind them. Her nerves threatened to reach the surface, but she blocked them out. She wanted this. Wanted *him*.

Derek strode into the en suite bathroom, set her down just inside the door, then pushed her up against it. Ginger looked up into his face and for once, forgot to hide her emotions. He'd adhered to her request without a moment's hesitation, simply because she'd asked. He would never know how much the small gesture meant to her. No one would hear them in the tiled room tucked in the back of the apartment. He was too busy undressing to acknowledge her gratitude, however.

As he untucked the white dress shirt from his pants, she caught a glimpse of his ridged abdomen before he let it drop. Her breathing roughened when he removed his shirt, exposing his stomach, arms, and chest. Derek had the kind of body that looked capable of inflicting pain and pleasure equally. His scattered tattoos made him look like a barroom brawler who bloodies half the men in the room but still has enough stamina afterward to satisfy two women in bed. His muscles shifted with every breath, like they could break free of his skin at any moment. He intimidated and aroused.

"Strip," he said.

His tone warned her not to protest. She didn't want to. Before she lost her courage, Ginger reached around and unzipped the dress, letting it slide down over her hips to pool at her feet, completely exposing her body to him. She pressed her palms against the door behind her so she wouldn't be tempted to cover herself.

Derek paused in the act of unbuckling his belt, his green eyes darkening until they appeared almost black. Her body readied further under his starved look. "Christ. I wish I had enough self-control to taste every inch of you."

He pushed his pants and boxer briefs down his legs, stepped out of them, and moved toward Ginger so fast, she gasped. Back pressed against the door, she let her gaze drop to the hand gripping his heavy erection, stroking it from root to head.

"Are you wet enough for me, Ginger?"

Before she could answer, he guided his cock between her slightly parted thighs and through her cleft, dragging the head achingly slow through her wetness. He growled near the top of her head, circling her clitoris with the engorged head. But he pulled himself away just as quickly, making Ginger whimper in protest.

He produced a condom and slid it down his imposing length. Then he dropped his hands to Ginger's ass and lifted her against him, lodging her between his body and the door. "Wrap your legs around my waist."

He groaned when Ginger did as he asked, cradling his erection with her softness. "The first time is going to be hard and fast. Do you understand? This is what you do to me."

Then he pushed inside her with such force, the door behind her shook on its hinges. Tears sprang to Ginger's eyes and she cried out, the sound mingling with Derek's strangled groan. Pain sliced through her, sharp and quick. Clinging to his shoulders, she prayed for the discomfort to subside as their harsh breathing echoed through the still bathroom.

Derek froze against her, chest heaving. His eyes held the unspoken question. Completely stripped of her defenses, she couldn't hide the answer.

Regret washed over his features. "Oh baby, *no*."

"Please," she gasped. "I don't want you to stop."

His voice sounded strangled. "Do you really think I could now, even if I wanted to?"

His already-stiff muscles bunched under her fingers as she stroked his neck and shoulders. Having Derek stop now when they'd come this far would devastate her. She laid kisses along his collarbone and his neck, entreating him to continue.

Despite the sting she'd experienced when he first thrust into her, the way his erection filled her so completely thrilled Ginger. There was pleasure to be found in the pain, she discovered. Impaled by Derek's hips against the hard surface of the door, Ginger shifted slightly in an effort to assuage the building ache.

"*Hold still.*" Punctuating his order, Derek's hips drove her into the door once more with a powerful thrust. "Fuck. *Fuck*. Just give me a goddamn minute."

"No. I *can't*. Derek…*please*." Her thoughts had scattered with the movement of his body inside hers and disjointed words began to fall from her lips. The pain remained, but she found it manageable when paired with the promise of something more just beginning to present itself. Still sensitive from her own touch during the car ride, she knew that if she could just move a certain way against Derek, she could use his body to find release.

Ignoring his request to remain still, she circled her hips over Derek's, moaning without restraint when that needy part of her slid against the smooth base of his erection buried deep inside her. She tightened her thighs around him and worked her lower body into a rhythm, concentrating on finding her pleasure. She felt wild. Starved. For him. For this. She wanted to slow down and savor the moment, but her body wouldn't allow it. Only a few more grinds of her hips… Her head fell back on her shoulders, anticipating her climax.

Derek's hands gripped her bottom, his fingers digging in painfully. The friction she'd craved was taken from her and she moaned in protest, pulling on his hair in frustration.

"No, no, you tight little virgin. I'm not going to let you off so easily. We've barely gotten started."

Holding her body still against him, Derek dipped his head and took one of her nipples in his mouth and drew on it greedily. Hot pleasure shot through Ginger, spreading through her belly and lower. She desperately needed to move, to rediscover her rhythm, but Derek wouldn't allow it. After licking and sucking her nipple to a peak, he moved to her other breast and gave it the same torturous yet reverent treatment. Ginger moved restlessly against the hard surface of the door, needing him to stop. Needing him to *never* stop.

Derek raised his head, his heated eyes landing on her lips and staying there, pupils dilating. His breathing escalated with each passing second.

"Give me your mouth. I want your mouth."

She pressed her forehead against his. "Then what are you waiting for?"

His lips fell on hers with a growl, biting, soothing, and licking. Their tongues met and tangled furiously. He forced her mouth open over and over again, demanding to be let inside. Head slanting right, then left, Ginger let the kiss consume her, never once thinking to come up for air. As he dominated her mouth, any lingering pain disappeared, replaced with single-minded need. He felt hot and thick inside her, and her body relaxed to accommodate his size.

At some point during the kiss, Derek braced one arm against the door, wrapped the other around her waist, and began moving Ginger up and down his rigid length, slowly torturing her slick, sensitive flesh. The pace grew faster and more determined until she bounced up and down on his erection. Derek's mouth never left hers, absorbing her cries with his tongue and lips.

Without warning, the pressure building inside Ginger burst and an immense wave of pleasure washed over her. She broke the kiss and screamed, dimly aware that Derek was watching her come apart in his arms as she rode out her orgasm with the use of his still-thrusting body.

When she finished, Derek buried his face in her neck with a groan. "I'm ruined. You've ruined me, Ginger."

With one final thrust of his hips, Derek found his release. He tried to muffle his shouts against her damp skin, but they couldn't be contained, and Ginger was too slack with pleasure to mind the expletives he chanted against her ear.

When they finally got their breathing under control, Derek shifted her body around so that he could loop his arms under her knees. He gathered her against his chest, carried her into the bedroom, and lay her down on the bed. Body limp, she watched as he returned to the bathroom and came back carrying a damp washcloth.

Derek kneeled in front of her and pressed the warm cloth between her legs. The heat soothed the remaining sting, leaving a sense of contentment in its wake. She watched through half-closed eyes as he ran the cloth along her inner thighs and back up.

When he'd finished his task, Derek tossed the cloth on his bedside table and began trailing kisses down Ginger's stomach.

Her eyes flew open as the intense sensations she'd just experienced rushed back to the surface. "Derek?"

His warm breath drifted over her most intimate place. "Quiet, baby. Just let me kiss it better."

Then he gently licked her to a second orgasm.

Chapter Fourteen

Ginger had been sipping a mug of coffee in Derek's kitchen and staring off into space for close to an hour when Willa startled her by coming out of the spare bedroom. Ginger glanced at her sister, then quickly averted her eyes, positive everything that transpired the night before showed on her face. And even if she tried to hide the myriad emotions fighting their way out of her chest, she'd never been able to hide a damn thing from Willa.

He'd left without a word.

As she'd lain there awake wondering what kind of awkward morning-after speech Derek had prepared, he'd left his bedroom—to take a shower, she'd assumed—and never returned. Waltzed right out the front door, leaving her wearing nothing but her birthday suit in his bed. She'd sat up like a shot at the realization that he'd left, surprised to find she would have preferred the awkward speech in exchange for how she now felt. Empty, exposed.

A little used.

She resented being made to feel that way. He wasn't

required to tell her she was special or cook her an omelet, but anything would have been preferable to silence. Silence could be interpreted to mean too many things. Maybe now that he'd gotten what he wanted from her, leaving without saying good-bye had been his way of gently nudging her toward the door.

Well, she'd be more than happy to oblige him.

Ginger grabbed her mug and went to rinse it out in the sink, giving her an excuse to turn her back. She felt the hot sting of tears behind her eyes, but blinked them away and focused on what needed to be done.

"Good news, sis," she called over her shoulder. "I called Lenny and since it's going to take a while to repair our place, he's letting us move into a vacant unit upstairs. I was thinking of browsing the local swap meet for pieces today, but I think I'd rather get a jump start on moving out of here and into the other place."

She didn't need to turn around to see Willa's confusion. It made no sense, swapping one temporary home for another. All she knew for certain? She needed to get out now. This moment. She didn't know how to explain that to Willa, though. Or herself for that matter.

"Why the rush? Why don't we just stay here instead of moving twice?"

"No reason," she said quickly. "Just want our own space."

The long pause that followed made Ginger's shoulder blades itch. "Are you sure it doesn't have anything to do with last night?"

Ginger tensed, then began cleaning the coffee mug for the third time. "What do you mean?"

"You and the lieutenant weren't exactly quiet about it," Willa said jokingly. "But hey, if you want to hit him and quit him, that's fine by me. We'll leave today."

Ginger's stomach plummeted to the floor. *No, please, no.*

She'd been careful, hadn't she? They'd been in the farthest room in the house. Had she been so caught up in the moment that she'd actually woken her little sister? *Just like...* She couldn't let the thought fully form or she would be ill.

Slowly, she turned from the sink to face her sister. "Oh God, Willa."

Her sister's smile disappeared and she came toward her with hands outstretched. "Ginger, come on. I was just kidding. Your side of the bed hasn't been slept in and you're sitting there stewing, so I took a wild guess. But I didn't hear anything. Honestly."

Ignoring Willa's attempts at denial, she breezed past her toward the bedroom.

"I'm going to pack. We'll be out of here today. I promise."

. . .

"I'd appreciate any information you can pass on." Derek lowered his voice as he strode down the hallway toward his apartment with a bag of groceries under his arm Monday evening. Adjusting the cell phone against his ear, he repeated the information. "Haywood Devon. Owns a few strip clubs in Nashville, among his other enterprises. I'm specifically interested in any connection he has with a Valerie Peet. Thanks."

Derek walked through his door and came to a stop. Staring down at the spare set of apartment keys resting on his kitchen counter, an uncomfortable feeling spread through his chest. He'd given Ginger the set when she and Willa moved into the spare bedroom Saturday night. Obviously at some point between Sunday morning and now, they'd left. Without giving him a courtesy call or leaving a simple note.

A muscle flexed in his jaw as he set down his phone a bit too heavily on the counter. He supposed he couldn't expect a courtesy call from Ginger when he'd neglected to do the same. Every time he'd picked up the phone to call her, he'd hung up, not knowing how to say what was on his mind. He had very little experience expressing his feelings to a woman, especially a woman like Ginger whose reactions he could never predict. No, what he wanted to say would need to be said face-to-face.

Derek hadn't slept or eaten a decent meal since Saturday night and until just now, when he walked through the door, he hadn't realized how much he'd needed Ginger to be here when he got home. Work had been hell now that Alvarez's informant had finally come through with information about a meeting between the two feuding gangs that was set to take place tomorrow night. He'd worked around the clock to get his men in place, organizing the raid and casing the location of the meet so they would know the lay of the land going in.

Those bastards were going down tomorrow night.

For two days, when he wasn't strategizing or running back and forth to police headquarters to brief the chief of police on their progress, he'd thought of Ginger nonstop. Every time he earned a quiet moment, she materialized in his mind looking like she had Sunday morning in his bed. Rosy and naked, snuggled into his pillows. The image was permanently seared into his brain and refused to fade. He didn't want it to.

She'd been a virgin. He still couldn't wrap his mind around it. Besides her age, an age when most woman had accumulated a decent number of partners, the way she moved, smiled, *breathed*—it oozed sensuality. He'd hated every man who'd made her that way, even though her outrageously sexy demeanor undeniably drew him in. He couldn't fathom a woman like Ginger, who left men drooling in her wake, making it to twenty-three without having been with a man.

He'd been her first. The first man to enter her body and

bring her to orgasm. He could still feel the way she'd tightened and shook around him so powerfully, as if she'd been waiting for *him* all that time, needing *him* to fill her and satisfy her. God, he'd never forget the way she'd moved and twisted on him like she couldn't get enough.

The things he'd said to her, *done* to her when she'd been inexperienced intruded on his conscience. If he'd known from the beginning that she was a virgin, would he have still spoken to her in that manner?

Yes, he realized. If that made him a bastard, so be it. Innocent or not, he found keeping himself in check around Ginger impossible, her positive reactions only encouraging him.

When he told her she'd ruined him, he meant it. He couldn't go back to the time before he knew what she tasted like, felt like, sounded like as he moved inside her. He'd changed her irrevocably on Saturday night and she'd done the same to him.

If she was trying to send him a message by leaving behind his keys and moving out without a word, he didn't like it. It made him anxious. An unfamiliar feeling for him. Something about the keys tossed so casually on the counter felt *final*. And their association was far from over.

Derek threw the entire bag of groceries in the refrigerator to deal with later and left the apartment. He strode down the hall to Ginger's door and knocked briskly.

A minute later when no one answered, he went to knock again when a throat cleared down the hall to his right. He turned and saw Willa standing halfway up the staircase, looking down at him with her default *what the fuck* expression. "You knocked?"

He looked between her and the apartment door. "What are you doing upstairs?"

She inspected her nails. "We moved into an empty unit

until they can fix ours."

What the fuck? "Why?"

She shrugged in response.

Clearly, he would get nowhere with Willa this century. "Is your sister home?"

"Nope."

"Where the hell is she?"

"On a date."

Derek's chest constricted so unpleasantly he couldn't breathe for a moment. Then he grew furious. A date? A fucking *date*? He'd find out where the hell she'd gone and with whom. Then he'd go there and kill the motherfucker.

He gripped the doorframe and contemplated ripping it off.

"Relax, man. She's just working at the bar. But for a second there, I bet you probably wished you'd called her at least once since Sunday."

The relief staggered him. If he thought he'd been possessive of Ginger before, it had just graduated to an entirely new level. A dangerous one. He needed to see her, but under the circumstances it would be wise to give himself some time to cool off. In his present state, he wouldn't be able to have a rational conversation about why she'd moved out. He'd only make things worse.

He took a deep breath and forced himself to smile. "Nicely done, Willa."

She gestured for him to follow her up the stairs. "I try."

When Derek walked into the third-floor apartment, he encountered Ginger everywhere. Her cowboy boots leaning up against the wall, various furniture pieces she'd decorated, the damn statue. *How had they gotten that thing up the flight of stairs?* The smaller two-bedroom smelled like freshly dried paint and lacked the homey feel of their downstairs apartment. It felt temporary, with scattered furniture and boxes stacked everywhere. Did she really prefer this situation to his apartment? The thought bothered him a great deal.

He turned to Willa. "So she left because I didn't call her?"

"Partially."

"Ginger is a grown-up," he said with a frown. "She doesn't need me holding her hand."

She rounded on him, reminding him of her sister. "That's right. She *is* a grown-up and has been for a very long time. She's also a girl."

What did that even mean? Derek tried to suppress a rising sense of panic and failed. "Wait. You said partially. Why else did she leave?"

Willa sank down in a kitchen chair with a heavy sigh. "It's partly my fault. I let her think I'd heard you guys, um, *doing your thing* on Saturday night. I didn't," she added quickly. "I just wanted her to fess up. It was obvious that something happened. She was acting funny."

He stared at her, unable to believe he was having this conversation with a seventeen-year-old. Then he remembered Ginger begging him at the door to be quiet so her sister wouldn't hear them. He hadn't recalled her vehement request until just now. "Why is it…such a huge issue for her?"

Willa looked uncomfortable, like she didn't want to answer. She buried her face in her hands with a groan. "Oh, for fuck's sake. It's like I'm doomed to talk about this all day. Ginger and I were fine until you two assholes came along."

Derek bristled. "What are you talking about? There's someone else? You said she was working, *dammit*."

She waved off his question. "There's no one else. I'm talking about my…this guy…never mind. You need to get yourself under control, man."

"Explain."

Willa stood, pacing around the table toward the window.

"Ginger would have an issue with me hearing you guys because of our mother. She used to turn tricks in our living room."

His face paled. "Shit."

"Yeah. Shit." She stared out the window, her back to Derek. "Ginger used to stuff cotton in my ears and blast country music to drown it out. She knew how much it upset me. That's why she has an issue with it now. She doesn't realize it only bothered me back then because I didn't understand it. To her, it's just plain black and white."

Derek had seen Valerie Peet's criminal record, not that he could tell Willa that. He'd known Ginger's childhood had more than likely been rough. Obviously, he hadn't even scratched the surface. Rage flowed through him just imagining two young girls being subjected to something so awful. Indeed, Ginger had been required to grow up at a very young age.

He sat down heavily in the kitchen chair vacated by Willa. "I still feel like I'm missing something."

She faced Derek across the table. "Our mother...she's complicated. Sometimes her johns would stick around for a few days. They'd make promises to her and then bail once the drugs dried up. She'd get depressed, go on a drinking binge." Willa plopped onto the back of the couch, crossing her arms over her middle. "I think you care about my sister, Lieutenant, so I'm going to drop some knowledge on you."

He managed a nod.

"I'm sure I don't have to remind you how attractive Ginger is. But so was our mother at one time. And Ginger's biggest fear has always been becoming our mother."

"Impossible."

Willa made a sound of agreement. "Still. It's the real reason she doesn't date. She watched men use our mother and discard her like yesterday's trash her whole life. So you see, you literally could not have fucked up more by bailing and not calling Ginger for two days."

Derek's throat felt banded by steel. Jesus, how could he not have realized this? She'd needed words, assurances from him, and he'd left without even saying good-bye. And, worse, stayed away while he let his work consume him without sending her so much as a text. Of course she'd feel insecure about where they stood. He'd given her no reason to feel otherwise. But what would he have said?

Thanks for the hottest fuck of my life, baby. Let's do it again as soon as I get home from work. Twice.

He scrubbed a hand over his face. Just as she'd been innocent of men, he lacked experience being in an actual relationship.

If he didn't want to lose her, he needed to figure it out. Fast.

He just hoped like hell it wasn't too late.

"I've got to get out of here."

"I thought you might."

...

"Aw, come on now, sugar tits. I've been tipping you all night. Show me something."

Ginger ignored the light-beer-drinking Neanderthal she'd nicknamed Nacho addressing her from the end of the bar, completely unaware of the tortilla chip stuck to his shirt. Subtly, she checked for the security guards in the crowd, hoping they'd come remove this guy quick. She'd alerted them over ten minutes ago that one of her customers needed tossing out, but they appeared to have forgotten or just plain blown her off. Any other night, she would brazen it out. Banter with the sorry fucker until he walked away or got too drunk to respond. It would probably even entertain the other patrons and increase her tips.

But he'd caught her on a bad night. A real bad night. And honestly, she could think of nothing more satisfying right now than gulping down each of her customers' drinks shotgun-style and line-dancing on the bar.

What the hell is this techno music about anyway? Everyone's just pretending to like it, right?

"Baby, you look mad. Don't be like that."

Ginger squeezed her eyes shut, wishing Neander-Nacho hadn't called her *baby*. It reminded her of Derek and their one-night stand. Their truly amazing one-night stand that would never be repeated, obviously, since he hadn't bothered to call or stop by once since it had happened. Seemed pretty damn clear where they stood.

The fact that she'd been a virgin probably scared the hell out of him, made him run for the hills thinking she'd be all clingy. Ready to go eat brunch and pick out a puppy.

Fat chance. She ate breakfast, or she ate lunch. The two had no business being combined.

Apart from Willa finding out, Ginger refused to regret it, though. In fact, when she saw Derek again, she might even wink and blow him a kiss. Just to let him know how much *non*-regretting she was doing.

She'd known from the beginning where this thing between Derek and her was headed and she'd gone there willingly. Eagerly. Sans panties, even. She didn't want a relationship with him. With anyone. So why had her bravado deserted her when she needed it most? She couldn't stop moping around like one of the characters in some scripted teen drama. Frankly, she was kind of embarrassed for herself.

It reminded her too much of someone. She'd been avoiding admitting it, but thanks to Neander-Nacho's antics, she'd started hanging streamers and blowing up balloons at her own pity party. She glanced up from the cash register and caught sight of herself in the mirror behind the bar. The dull, defeated girl she saw there terrified her.

"Sweetheart, I'm *talking* to you. Not that I don't mind seeing you from behind." High fives, the clinking of glasses against one another.

Dull and defeated, my ass.

Ginger spun around and approached the jackass who no longer deserved a nickname. She spoke loud enough for anyone within earshot to hear. "Listen, you ignorant bastard, I have some news for you. There are literally *dozens* of loser, backward-hat-wearing, fart-joke-telling sons of bitches exactly like you in this establishment right now. You are not unique in any way. In fact, you are boring the shit out of me with your predictability. So finish your goddamn drink and pack it up."

Then she picked up his untouched shot of tequila and tossed it back, reveling in the burn as it flowed down her throat.

The handful of patrons who could hear her tirade over the pounding music applauded and whistled for her. Even the guy's friends poked him, repeating the highlights of her put-down. He didn't look happy about it in the least. His face turned bright red, his fist clenching on the bar. Slightly alarmed, Ginger turned back around, intending to call for security once more.

A hand banded around her bicep, yanking her backward. The wooden bar bit into her upper back and her leg slammed into a sharp corner of the ice bin. She struggled to pull her arm from his hand to no avail. His friends shouted at him to let go, but his grip merely tightened.

"You're a whore!" He yelled against her ear. She flinched at the volume of his voice. In a panic, she swung her eyes to the other end of the bar, where Amanda jogged toward her wide-eyed, dropping the drink she'd been pouring on the way to reach her.

Suddenly Ginger's arm ripped free of his grasp and she slumped to the floor, hidden from view behind the bar. A loud crash, followed by shouting coming from the dance floor, had her scrambling to her feet.

Ginger's eyes widened. Derek stood behind Nacho, gripping him around the throat with murder in his eyes.

Chapter Fifteen

Nacho's hands tore at Derek's grip, trying to free his neck so he could breathe. Likewise, Nacho's friends appeared frantic, trying to pull Derek away from Nacho, but he wouldn't budge.

Derek's turbulent gaze met hers briefly and she read his silent question there. She nodded at him once to assure him she was unharmed. Then without warning, he slammed Nacho's head against the bar with such force that Ginger jumped back to escape the blood spurting from his nose. Even the crunch of cartilage breaking could be heard over the pulsing music.

"Derek, no! Stop!"

The club had ground to a halt, everyone turning to see what the disturbance was about. Customers moved back and out of the way as Derek pulled Nacho off the bar and launched him onto the ground, then straddled his neck, clearly intending to continue the one-sided fight. Ginger knew she had to take action or Derek would seriously injure the other man.

Using the ice machine for leverage, she leaped on the bar

and jumped down on the other side. She winced at the pain in her right leg, but pushed forward through the gaping club-goers to throw herself on Derek's back. Ginger wrapped her arms around his chest, dug in her feet, and pulled to no avail. He still landed a punch squarely in Nacho's face and reared back to hit him once more. She grabbed his arm and held on with all her might.

"Listen to me! You need to stop!" Out of the corner of her eye, Ginger saw the club's two burly security guards pushing their way through the crowd. Thankfully, a different fight had just broken out between two girls and drew the guards' attention away from Derek.

As pissed as she felt, it occurred to her that Derek, being a police lieutenant, would definitely not benefit from being involved in a bar fight. She needed to get him out of the club before the guards realized the real fight was on her side of the bar and tried to detain him. In his current irrational state, he might even fight back and the situation would only escalate.

She put her mouth against his ear and tried to reason with him. "Derek, please. I'm fine. You need to stop right now. You are going to kill him. I'm fine."

His body shook with adrenaline. "He had his hands on you."

"It's my fault. I provoked him. But it's over now."

Derek turned his head and met her eyes. "Your *fault*?"

She flinched at his fury. Out of the corner of her eye, she saw the security guards parting the sea of club-goers, nearly upon them. As an employee, she would have a better chance of getting Derek out of the bar without being held up by security.

And he *had* been defending her. Despite his extreme and unnecessary methods, a tiny part of her felt grateful that after years of inexcusable behavior from male customers, someone besides her had finally stepped in and put a stop to it. No accounting for subtlety.

"Get your shit."

Ginger recoiled. She'd already made the choice to leave with him, but his high-handed tone infuriated her, made her want to change her mind. "You can't just demand I leave in the middle of my shift!"

"I can shut this place down with one phone call. Give me a reason to do it. Please."

Anger rapidly building inside of her, she shot to her feet. Nacho writhed on the floor in front of him, hands clutching his shattered nose. Beside her, Derek growled. He'd noticed the bleeding cut on her leg and looked ready to turn on Nacho once more.

The security guards reached Derek then, but he extricated his badge and barked something at them before they made the mistake of touching him. He turned to her, his eyes nearly black with fury. "Ginger. Get. Your. Shit."

She turned toward the bar and signaled Amanda. Already having anticipated her request, the other woman tossed Ginger her purse, which she'd stashed in a cabinet beneath the register. Ginger mouthed a thank-you just as Derek put a hand on her back, then steered her, through their rapt audience, toward the door.

"Where is your coat?"

"In the back room," she snapped. "You didn't exactly give me enough time to go get it."

He whipped off his jacket and settled it on her shoulders just as they exited the club into the cold Chicago evening. Smokers hung around in packs outside, oblivious to the scene that had just taken place inside the club. Ginger vaguely registered the bouncer at the door calling her name questioningly before Derek boosted her into the passenger seat of his SUV.

They didn't speak on the ride home, the air thick and

tense between them. Derek gripped the steering wheel tightly under knuckles smeared with blood, a muscle ticking dangerously in his jaw.

His obvious anger only fueled Ginger's. The second they pulled up in front of the building, she jumped out of the car and slammed the door, stomping toward the building without looking back. She sensed Derek right behind her as she turned her key to unlock the front door to the building, but she refused to acknowledge him. When they reached the third floor, she flung off his jacket and threw it over her shoulder at him without breaking stride toward her temporary apartment.

She heard Derek's dark laughter behind her. "We can have it out in your place or mine, Ginger. It doesn't matter to me. But it happens tonight."

"Fuck you."

"Inevitably."

Ginger froze outside her door. If she ignored him and went inside, she would fume until the sun came up, imagining all the insults she could have thrown at him. A fight would be infinitely more satisfying.

She marched back down the stairs toward Derek's place. No way would she wake Willa up with an argument between her and Derek. Furthermore, she didn't want her sister knowing what had taken place tonight at Sensation. It would upset her.

He wants a fight? I'll give him one to remember.

Derek unlocked the door and gestured for Ginger to precede him inside, which she did with a toss of her hair. After flipping on the overhead light, she flung her purse on his kitchen table and faced him. He was looking for something under his kitchen sink, which he eventually found. A first-aid kit.

Ginger scowled over his concerned gesture. She'd come

here for a fight, *dammit.*

"All right, Derek. You proved tonight you had the biggest dick in the room. You've clubbed me over the head and brought me back to your cave. Where do you want me? We don't even have to be quiet this time." She hopped up on the kitchen table and lifted her shirt. "How about right here on the table? Or maybe the couch?"

Derek took two quick strides toward her and slammed the metal box down on the table. He pulled the hem of her shirt back down before it reached her breasts. But not before she saw a familiar hunger tighten his features. "All right, you've made your point."

"Really? I feel like I haven't even started." Her eyes flashed with heat. "What were you doing at Sensation tonight?"

"I came to see you."

"Why?"

"You damn well shouldn't have to ask me that." Uncharacteristic regret flashed across his features. "Look, Ginger, I should have called you. Or at least said good-bye Sunday morning. The fact that I was practically handcuffed to my desk for two days is no excuse. I handled this badly."

Her eyes widened in surprise. "Handled *what* badly, Derek? There is nothing here. We had sex. People do it all the time. I don't need you to write me a poem."

"It was your first time." Anger infused his tone. "You deserved more than a quick fuck against my bathroom door."

How *dare* he tell her what she deserved? He didn't know what growing up with Valerie had been like. Watching her mother's self-worth wither or thrive, depending on who occupied her bed. She'd made the decision at a young age never to give *anyone* the power to destroy her ability to reason. That included the man standing in front of her.

Ginger leaned forward, getting right in his face. "*I* decided when, where, and with whom my first time happened. No one made that decision for me. And I don't regret it. I'm sorry if you do. Won't let it happen again."

"Don't put words in my mouth. I don't regret it. I'll *never* regret it. I just wish you would have told me." He brushed the hair off her shoulder, his fingers lingering against her skin. "I could have hurt you, baby."

The Derek who hadn't called her for two days then started a bar brawl vanished, replaced by the gentle, caring Derek who scared her so much more. Recognizing the shift in his demeanor, she pushed his hand away in panic and tried to slide off the table.

He gripped her legs until she stopped struggling, then knelt down in front of her with the first-aid kit.

She stared at the top of his head, dumbfounded. "What is this? What are you doing?"

Derek began cleaning the wound on her leg with peroxide and cotton. "I'm taking care of your cut before it gets infected."

"No. That's not what I meant. I don't *need* this from you, Derek. Do you have some misplaced sense of guilt because you bagged a virgin? Because you shouldn't." She banged her fist on the table to get his attention. He ignored her, produced a bandage, and applied it on top of her injury. "Stop this bullshit! I don't need you to pretend you want me for more than sex."

Derek shot to his feet, looming furiously above her. "You have no idea what I want."

Except, she did. And, oh God, he really meant it. He wanted her. And not just for her body. She could see it in his face, hear it in his words. How had she gotten here?

Push him away.

"What if *I* don't want more with *you*? Did you even consider that?"

"If you didn't want more with me, Ginger, you wouldn't have made me your first."

Her laughter came out sounding hysterical. "God, you're so fucking arrogant. You think I want to be your girlfriend or something?"

Jaw clenched, Derek rose from the floor to toss the bandage wrapper in the trash can. "I don't care what you call yourself. Titles are irrelevant to what I want with you."

Ginger stared at his retreating back, trying to stop his words from sinking in, from taking hold. *What I want with you.* Everything she thought she'd known an hour ago had been tossed out the window. He wanted more from her than a one-night stand, but what did *more* entail? A month? A year? Once it ended and he moved on, Ginger imagined it would be like taking the way his noncommunication had made her feel over one weekend and multiplying it by a hundred.

No, thank you.

One little problem remained, however.

She still wanted him.

Ginger watched Derek move around the kitchen, unstrapping his shoulder holster and removing his gun. Her heart kicked up the pace as he untucked his shirt, giving her a glimpse of his tight stomach. Oh God, she needed him *inside* her. Once hadn't been nearly enough to extinguish the fires he'd stoked.

Could she have it both ways? Sex without commitment? *Men* were supposed to be the ones who wanted that, right? Perhaps as long as their relationship remained physical, Ginger could resist developing any kind of feelings for him. Eventually, she would work Derek out of her system for good. He'd probably need very little convincing to see things her way. She still wasn't entirely convinced his guilt over taking her virginity didn't drive the argument.

He just needs a little convincing that this relationship

business isn't necessary.

She tugged down the neckline of her top, then slipped off the table to sway toward Derek. His head whipped around, as if sensing the shift in her attitude, and watched her approach through wary eyes.

She paused in front of him, hoping the look she gave him was contrite. "I'm sorry, Derek. I don't want to fight." She ran a finger down the row of buttons on his shirt, playing with the final one against his lower stomach. "Not when we could be doing something else."

When he could no longer resist looking down at her cleavage, Ginger felt a jolt of satisfaction at the way his Adam's apple bobbed in his throat. "I know what you're doing. It's not going to work."

"What am I doing? Seducing you?" She reached down with one hand and undid the button on her black shorts, letting them slip down her legs to reveal her lacy pink underwear. "Is it working now?"

She watched him fight a losing battle to keep his eyes locked on hers. His hooded gaze traveled down her stomach, over her hips and legs, lingering on the triangle of lace between her thighs. His tortured groan shot heat straight to her core. "*Fuck,* baby."

When he still didn't reach for her, Ginger's nimble fingers began working the buckle of his belt. She might be inexperienced, but she'd worked in a bar ever since she'd turned sixteen and lied about her age to get the job. You learned a thing or two about men when you spent your days and nights liquoring them up. Word on the street had always been that a man's decisions were made with *this* head, not the one on top of his shoulders.

She listened to Derek's breath accelerate as she unhooked the leather and slid it through the loops. It dropped to the floor with a *clack*.

Ginger looked up at him through her eyelashes, daring him to tell her not to continue. Apart from the roughening breath puffing against her forehead, Derek remained silent, his green eyes trained on her hands. She slid down the zipper of his pants. In the quiet kitchen, the zipping noise was amplified. It sounded terribly erotic to her ears.

"I'm trying really hard here," he panted. "I won't be able to stop soon."

"Why would you stop? I don't want you to."

"You know why. We're more than sex, Ginger. Accept it."

Her heart squeezed, but she kept an innocent expression on her face. She slipped her hand inside his pants and boxer briefs to close her fingers around his straining erection, molding him in her hand.

"Please, I want you so bad."

His breath hissed out through his teeth. "Oh, God. I want you, too. So fucking bad, sweetheart."

Then why was he being so damn stubborn? Surely he wouldn't reject her advances over some doomed attempt at a relationship. Couldn't he see it would never last? Nothing ever lasted when you put faith in anyone besides yourself. She tried to keep the desperation off her face. If he fought against this much longer, she didn't want to ponder where that left her.

Ginger stood on tiptoes and placed openmouthed kisses along his neck, all the while stroking him against her palm. "Do you want to put it in my mouth, Derek?" she whispered against his ear.

"*Jesus Christ.*"

"You'll be my first. Don't you want to be my first again?"

"Enough! That's fucking enough." Clenching his teeth, he took her wrist and removed the hand fondling his erection, groaning as he freed himself.

Then he pinned her body against the refrigerator and

brought his mouth down on hers, hard. Her eager mouth opened under his, letting his tongue sweep inside and take ownership. He wrapped her long hair around his fist, pulling with just the right amount of force and angling her head to accept his onslaught. Ginger's hands were pinned above her head in Derek's stronger grip, held there as his mouth doled out punishment. She accepted it greedily and without hesitation.

Arousal mixed with relief. He hadn't rejected her. Ginger's head swam with a multitude of unnamed emotions, overwhelming her senses. She could feel his raging need pressing against her stomach and squirmed against it, telling him without words how ready she was for him.

Then the kiss changed. His hips slowly distanced themselves from hers, the delicious friction disappearing. The hands manacling hers dropped lower to cup her face. Instead of being bruising and relentless, his tongue now soothed hers, as if apologizing for his earlier roughness. He brushed each of her swollen lips in turn, then left her mouth to dance across her face, planting soft kisses on her cheeks, eyelids, and forehead.

A sob broke from Ginger's throat. Tears she hadn't felt forming in her eyes cascaded down her cheeks. Derek kissed them away.

"Give me a chance, beautiful girl," he whispered urgently against her mouth.

Something inside Ginger shattered. Self-preservation had her pushing Derek away and frantically pulling on her discarded shorts. Her hands shook so violently, it took her a full minute to get them buttoned and zipped. She could feel Derek watching her the entire time but she refused to look at him, knowing instinctively that his expression would force her to accept something impossible.

Snatching her purse off the counter, she turned and

rushed to leave.

"Ginger, wait."

"Don't come anywhere near me, Derek. I don't want to see you anymore," she half-sobbed without turning around, then slammed the door.

Chapter Sixteen

Clip clip clip.

Ginger cut smoothly around the image of a giant duck and pasted it to the coffee table's surface, smoothing the edges with her fingers. It reminded her of the disastrous Halloween she attempted to dress up five-year-old Willa in a makeshift costume consisting of a pillowcase and flip-flops. The final touch had been an orange funnel she'd taped over her sister's mouth in lieu of a beak. They'd been forced to return home when Willa kept running into people and trees, unable to see over the kitchen utensil.

She turned the page in her *Good Housekeeping* magazine, eyes immediately drawn to the image of a family dressed in robes, gathered around a Christmas tree, complete with a wealth of wrapped presents at its base. Her smile disappeared. They'd never been able to afford a Christmas tree or presents, save the camera she'd bought Willa one year. Carefully, she cut around the tree, before applying paste to the back and slapping it upside down on the table, partially obscuring the picture of Dolly.

As she browsed further through the glossy pages, Ginger caught herself wondering what kind of home life Derek experienced as a child, then quickly sipped her scalding coffee to dispel the thought. She would never find out and it didn't matter. His childhood could have rivaled hers in shittiness and it wouldn't change a thing.

She ripped a page from the magazine and began cutting out a cherry pie recipe. Maybe this project's theme could be *Irony*. A table full of things they'd never had. Disgusted with her attitude, Ginger let the scissors drop on the floor and heaved the magazine across the room.

Ironic is me buying Good Housekeeping *magazine in the first place*, she thought, looking around at her pathetic attempt to create a home for Willa. It might have been a vast improvement from Nashville, but to her it screamed *low-class*. God, she'd never escape the reminders of where and what she'd come from. Maybe she wasn't meant to.

Ginger wrapped her arms around her knees and hugged them to her chest, letting her head fall forward. The second her eyes closed, Derek's plea swam through her mind.

Give me a chance, beautiful girl.

Was she only imagining the plaintiveness in his tone? She hadn't slept since their conversation, the memory still felt achingly fresh. Allowing herself to imagine, even for a second, what he'd meant by "give me a chance," left her feeling dizzy and panicked. He didn't know, *couldn't know*, what he asked of her.

By forcing her to acknowledge that his interest went beyond sexual attraction, he'd effectively blasted a hole in the side of her already-sinking ship. She didn't know her own identity without the illusion of sex. Had always used her looks to her advantage. But he wanted more. He wanted *her*.

Who am I, really?

Yesterday, she would have winked and told anyone who

asked, "I'm a Southern girl with a big heart and an even bigger mouth." Today? She didn't have an answer. For so long, her focus had been solely on Willa, and she wouldn't change her actions for anything in the world. But somewhere along the way, had she become the girl she'd merely been pretending to be?

Derek seemed to think more existed underneath the surface. How could he be so sure? If she gave him a chance, how long would it take him to realize his error?

She couldn't open herself up for that kind of pain.

Not even for Derek, who could comfort, arouse, and challenge with a single look.

Caught up in her own thoughts, Ginger nearly jumped out of her skin when Willa spoke to her from the kitchen.

"Coffee, sis?"

How long had she been standing there? "No thanks, I've already had three cups."

"Good lord." Willa scooped the grounds into the holder, added water, and closed the lid. "Who are you and what have you done to Ginger?"

"Huh?" Trying to hide her puffy eyes, Ginger looked down, concentrating on the cigarette advertisement she pasted on the coffee table.

Willa frowned as she removed a coffee mug from the cabinet. "You worked last night. Shouldn't you still be in bed?"

"Hmmm? Yeah. I couldn't sleep." She cleared the cobwebs from her throat and smiled at Willa. "Hey, I had an idea! I found this amazing coffee table downtown and I thought we could collaborate on it. We can combine some of your photos with the interesting clippings I find. It'll be ours when we finish. We'll keep it. What do you think?"

Willa finished pouring milk into the mug, then returned her smile. "I'll go get my portfolio. Maybe I have some old shots we can use."

"Great!"

Avoiding Willa's intelligent gaze, Ginger ducked her head once more, pretending to consider different placements for the cutout she held in her hand. A few minutes later, Willa came back in the room carrying an oversize folder and took up residence on the floor beside her. Ginger felt a rush of gratitude for her sister when she refrained from mentioning the overtly sarcastic quality of the project so far.

Willa extricated a handful of photographs and began picking through them.

Ginger set down the magazine and picked up a glossy eight-by-ten shot of a broad-shouldered young man wearing a basketball uniform, his brows drawn together in concentration. The players surrounding him were the only giveaway that he was a high school student, because of how much older he looked. "Who's this?"

"That's Evan. Evan Carmichael."

"Oh." Ginger studied the picture. "Did you take this on Friday night? It's really good, Wip."

"Yep, I did. Thanks."

Ginger set the photograph back down on top of the pile. "He's really cute. Do you know him?" She winced at her attempt to sound nonchalant. Willa would definitely clam up on the double.

"Yeah. I know him. Actually..." She tugged the sleeves of her hoodie over her wrists, poking her thumb through a hole she'd created. "I think he's going to ask me to the prom. Ha."

Ginger's mouth fell open. "Wh-what did you say? You're considering going to a *dance* with this boy?"

"I'm thinking about it. Yeah." She sighed. "*If* he asks, I'll go."

Ginger's mind reeled. Her little sister, who to the best

of her knowledge avoided human contact at all costs, had agreed to attend a dance? Remembering Willa's reaction to her barb about attending the school basketball game, Ginger refrained from relaying her thoughts aloud.

Did this mean coming to Chicago had been the right thing for Willa? She scrutinized the blush staining her sister's cheeks, the glimmer of humor in her eye. Ginger's heart swelled.

She quickly tried to hide her proud-mama reaction by ducking her head, but her smile must have shown because Willa snickered into her coffee cup.

"Well, that's fantastic, Willa," Ginger said, attempting casual. "I assume you'll need a dress?"

"I might."

"Then I *might* be able to help pick it out?"

Willa laughed. "Ginger, I know fuck-all about dresses. You're hired."

Unable to restrain herself, Ginger clapped her hands twice. "Great. Just give me a little direction. Short, long, strapless…?"

Her sister gave a lopsided smile. "Just make me look better than Evan's ex-girlfriend, Natalie. The blond, pom-pom-toting femme-bot."

Ah, so this is what had been bothering Willa. She felt a rush of relief. Normal teenage problems. "Girl, when I'm done, she'll have nothing on you."

They passed the next hour going through Willa's photographs and pulling out their favorites, deciding where to place them. Ginger even managed to weasel a few more details about Evan out of her sister—enough to get the sense that she really liked the boy. Which was shocking, to say the least. When Willa eventually left for school, Ginger dragged herself from the floor and went to make a fresh pot of coffee.

As she waited for it to brew, she tried to comprehend the last hour. Instead of reticent and moody, Willa had been practically jovial as they worked on the joint project. She'd had to force herself to act normal and not gape at the changes taking place in her sister. Her signature snark and foul mouth hadn't gone anywhere, which Ginger found herself oddly thankful for. She loved the old Willa just as much as the new one.

Sipping at her fresh cup, Ginger found herself torn between joy over Willa's transformation and confusion over her own inability to transform herself. Perhaps it had to do with age. Willa was still young and able to learn new tricks, so to speak. Ginger chose to take it as a sign that in some small way, she might have actually managed to shield Willa from the worst of their upbringing before it caused any permanent damage.

As for herself, she'd lacked any type of shield or voice of reason. Her life had been molded into a shape and left to harden in the sun. It was too late for her to change now.

Chapter Seventeen

After knocking one final time on Ginger's door and not getting an answer, Derek turned to leave with a frustrated curse. She wouldn't answer his phone calls and he didn't have time to sit and wait for her to get back from wherever she'd gone.

With the situation at work rapidly coming to a head, the last place he should've been was trying to track down an AWOL Ginger, but goddammit, he couldn't concentrate on the upcoming operation after the way they'd left things. She'd looked so shaken up leaving his apartment. If he could just talk to her, touch her, he would find a way to reassure her.

He'd walked into Sensation last night with every intention of humbling himself. He'd fucked up by allowing two days to pass with radio silence between them. Ginger might not admit it, but she'd needed him to make her feel wanted. And not just for one night. Instead, he'd gone off to work like an arrogant jackass, thinking she'd still be there playing house when he finally made it home. Sidling up to the bar, he'd been desperate to lay eyes on her after two days of missing her like hell.

The way she tilted her head when she back-talked him in that sexy accent. The way she pronounced his name. Her body fitting against his perfectly. Her scent. Her smile. He missed it all.

Then he'd seen that bastard's hands on her. Little flashes of light had sparked in front of his eyes before it all went red. He couldn't remember anything after that. Exiting the club and driving home was still a blur in his memory. With his blood still hot and pumping from the fight, he'd almost lost his control back at his apartment when she'd tried to seduce him. He still couldn't believe he'd walked away from that level of temptation.

Jesus, the things she'd said...

He released a shuddering breath.

Unfortunately, he now had a reason to be concerned about more than just their tenuous relationship. He'd uncovered something this weekend that had him actively worrying about her safety. In addition to the mountain of bureaucratic bullshit he'd shoveled through this week, he'd fit in some calls to Nashville and filled in some gaps about Valerie Peet. The word around Nashville was that she owed a large sum of money to heavy hitter, Haywood Devon.

Derek's sixth sense had started ticking once he received that information. Pieces were finally beginning to fall into place. Ginger leaving Nashville seemingly out of the blue, uprooting Willa so close to the end of her senior year. Her ability to afford an apartment well outside her means. The way she changed the subject whenever the past reared its head.

Ginger was in possession of the money.

She'd seen an opportunity to escape and taken it. Derek didn't blame her. In fact, he was grateful for her actions because they had brought her to Chicago. To him. But as their relationship stood now, he couldn't tell her he knew. She would panic and disappear, and he'd never see her again. The very prospect froze the blood in his veins.

Derek's pacing came to a halt when he heard footsteps coming up the stairs, hoping like hell for it to be Ginger. Instead, he saw Willa, shoulders hunched, looking completely distraught.

He cleared his throat to alert Willa of his presence and her head jerked up to reveal puffy, red-rimmed eyes. Embarrassment quickly followed, but then her chin went up a notch. Derek knew false bravado when he saw it. He also knew that if he showed her any kind of sympathy, she'd eat him alive. Apparently it ran in the family.

"Shouldn't you be at school?"

"Shouldn't you be at work?"

Derek shrugged. "Lunch break."

"Bullshit. Is Ginger not at home or is she just ignoring you?"

"Is ditching school a regular thing for you?"

"No. Maybe." She glared at him. "Why the hell do you care? You're a homicide cop, not a truancy officer."

"Just a concerned citizen is all."

Willa rolled her eyes and pushed past him. "If you're looking for a way to score points with my sister, try not being an epic douche bag."

Christ, this kid didn't pull any punches. He kind of admired it. "Okay, I deserve that."

He'd surprised her, but she hid it well. She kept her eyes down and dug around for her keys in her backpack. "Is there anything else I can help you with?"

"You can tell me why you look like shit."

She barked out a sarcastic laugh. "Oh, *now* I know what Ginger sees in you."

At least he'd gotten her to laugh. That counted for

something. Without Ginger there to deal with her sister, he felt the need to fix it. Only one problem: he had very little experience comforting teenagers. Best to stick with his tried and true good cop/bad cop method. "Listen"—he checked his watch—"I don't have time to watch some teenager cry and snot all over herself, but if you need to talk, I can pretend that I give a crap for a few minutes."

"Need to talk?" Her mouth dropped open. "I can't believe this. You're *handling* me."

"Sorry?"

"Lieutenant, you're smarter than I gave you credit for. How is it that you're so inept when it comes to handling my sister?"

"No one handles your sister."

She shrugged. "I'll concede that."

The sound of heels clicking on wood grabbed their attention seconds before Ginger came into view at the top of the stairs. Derek's mouth went dry at the sight of her. In jean shorts and cowboy boots, Ginger never looked less than stunning, but goddamn, she'd done something completely different today. Her hair had been pulled back away from her face and piled on top of her head in a loose bun. She wore a modest cream-colored dress that revealed no cleavage and dropped past her knees.

How then did she look the sexiest he'd ever seen her? He wanted to meet her halfway down the hall and kiss the breath out of her. Carry her into his apartment. Remind her how well he knew her body.

Derek heard Willa snicker at him behind his back. "Va va voom, sis. Who are you so dressed up for?"

Which had been his next fucking question.

When she spotted Willa standing behind him, Ginger's pace quickened, her black pumps tapping with each step. "Willa, thank God. Is everything okay? I just saw your missed call."

She passed Derek to get to her sister, shooting him a wary glance. Her wildflower scent washed over him. In that moment, he wanted very badly to be the first and last person each day to breathe it in.

"I'm fine, G."

He watched Ginger's own tired eyes widen as she examined her sister's appearance. Willa tried to convey her usual belligerent expression, but didn't quite pull it off. Her lower lip quivered a little.

"Is it the boy?" Ginger asked softly.

Willa burst into tears and launched herself into her sister's arms. Ginger, appearing stunned by her sister's show of emotion, stumbled backward a step before righting herself and tightening her arms around Willa.

A boy. He hadn't seen that one coming.

Ginger met Derek's gaze over her sister's shoulder, her eyes swimming with fear and uncertainty. He swallowed around the knot in his throat at seeing her so unsure. Deserted of her usual confidence. Nodding somberly, he tried to communicate with his eyes that everything would be all right. For now, it would have to be enough.

Another set of footsteps pounded up the staircase. He frowned when a boy the size of a linebacker appeared, looking panicked and out of breath. The kid's eyes widened on the girls embracing farther down the hallway, and with a choked noise, he tried to rush toward them past Derek. He stopped the newcomer cold with a firm hand to the chest.

"I'd explain myself rather quickly, if I were you."

He didn't even spare Derek a glance. "Willa, talk to me."

Derek looked back over his shoulder to see Ginger standing protectively in front of Willa, fury radiating from her gorgeous face. He could have stood there watching her all day. She turned slightly and whispered something to Willa before sailing forward, coming to a stop near Derek.

Derek watched the kid's eyebrows shoot skyward upon seeing Ginger up close. *I know that feeling too well.* To his credit, the kid kept his eyes from dropping below Ginger's neck.

"You must be Ginger."

"Oh? And why is that?" Her voice cracked like a whip and the kid winced. "Why *must* I be Ginger?"

"Willa mentioned that you...that everyone you meet falls in love with you. Not that *I* am," he rushed out. "I'm just saying, I can understand it. Other people doing it. Oh God, I can't say or do anything right today. Do you ever have a day like that? I am screwing this up so badly."

Some of the fight went out of Ginger. She raised an eyebrow at Derek, obviously thinking the same thing he did. This kid seemed like the furthest thing from a heartbreaker.

"And you *must* be Evan. The reason my little sister is so upset. I don't like to see my sister upset, Evan. Not at all. Give me one reason I shouldn't toss you out of here on your ass."

Evan looked relieved that Ginger was giving him an opportunity to speak. He tried to peek past her to see Willa, who stood immobilized at the end of the hallway, but Ginger blocked his view, crossing her arms over her chest. "I just need a chance to explain. She knows I would never hurt her on purpose. I just have to keep reminding her. And I will. Every day until she believes it."

Ginger's arms dropped to her sides, her anger deflating completely. *Damn, maybe this kid can give* me *some advice on how to handle a Peet sister.* After scrutinizing Evan for several long moments, Ginger turned and passed a silent question on to Willa, who lifted one shoulder and let it drop in response.

"All right, Evan. You have two minutes to make my sister smile before I turn you from a rooster to a hen in one shot. And don't think I can't do it."

They both watched as Evan approached Willa. When he'd made it halfway, Willa held up a hand signaling for him to stop, which he immediately did.

"Natalie ambushed me in the parking lot this morning," Evan began. "Her friends, my friends. Everyone was standing around talking. Out of nowhere she announces we're going to prom together. She knew I wouldn't correct her and embarrass her in front of everyone. She counted on it. I don't even know why she wants to go with me. We're barely even friends anymore."

Willa stayed silent, clutching the strap of her backpack against her chest. Derek couldn't tell by her expression whether or not she believed the poor kid. To be honest, he felt funny watching this teen drama play out, but he sensed Ginger needed him there. Even if she would never admit it.

"I did everything I could to find Natalie before fourth period, to tell her I wanted to ask you. I never even wanted you to know about what happened, but I didn't get to her in time. She knows now, though. Believe me."

Willa's face cracked. "I hate you for making me care about some stupid high school dance, Evan Carmichael."

He took a cautious step toward her. "No, you don't hate me. Don't say that."

Tears streaked down her face. "Yes, I do."

"Please don't cry. There's nothing to cry about." Evan reached Willa in two strides and lifted her off the floor into a sweeping hug. She stuck her damp face in the crook of his neck and sobbed.

Derek glanced down at Ginger, who watched the couple in complete awe, moisture brimming in her eyes. Derek reached out without thinking and stroked a thumb across her cheek to comfort her. She leaned into his palm for a moment, then flinched away.

Derek sighed. "I have to get back to work, but we need to

talk tomorrow."

"I don't think that's a good idea."

"Dammit, I—" His phone rang, cutting him off. Derek read the caller ID flashing across the screen. The chief of police had called twice, probably wondering where the hell he'd gone with less than an hour to go before the raid. "I have to go. We *will* talk tomorrow."

Derek couldn't afford to wait for her reply. He turned and stalked out of the building.

Chapter Eighteen

Ginger woke on the floor as if a fire alarm had gone off, knocking over a half-full glass of red wine.

What the hell is that noise?

She shoved the heels of her hands against her eyes, blocking out the lamplight. A magazine clipping depicting a cat wearing sunglasses was stuck to one of her hands, and she ripped it off, letting it flutter to the floor. When her momentary fuzziness passed, she tried to piece together the last few hours.

Willa and Evan reuniting in the hallway. Evan staying for dinner. Ginger watching Willa smile and laugh like she hadn't done in years while Ginger plied herself with wine, lamenting the fact that she was now the only emotionally stunted sister in the room.

Check, check, and check.

She buried her head in her hands and groaned. When had the world shifted and left her sitting in the same spot? They'd been fine before, hadn't they? Two sisters against the world! Sure, they never discussed their hopes or fears, but they sure as hell had each other's backs. Now, Ginger wondered if she'd been wearing blinders as her sister developed an entirely new facet to her personality.

She'd been the one to make the decision to leave Chicago for a new start, but the only thing she'd really changed was her location. Willa had found a way to move on from the past. Why couldn't she?

Derek wanted to talk to her tomorrow. The very idea of discussing a potential relationship between them frightened her. He didn't realize how impossible a task he faced trying to convince her to take that leap. Did he think a simple conversation could erase the previous twenty-three years she spent not trusting anyone but herself?

We're more than sex, Ginger. Accept it.

Oddly enough, she had accepted it. Something very clearly existed between them besides their intense sexual attraction. Otherwise, she wouldn't be feeling sexually frustrated, sitting in a pool of cheap wine. She'd be with Derek, working out those frustrations in a far more entertaining manner.

She couldn't allow herself to succumb to those urges, though. Every second she spent with him made it harder to keep a comfortable distance. And even if she wanted to attempt a purely sexual relationship with Derek, he'd made it clear that arrangement didn't work for him. Damn him for that. Because his restraint had accomplished far more than simply impressing her, which it had. It made her wonder if his intentions toward her really were genuine. If maybe a relationship could work if two strong-willed people, such as them, wanted it to.

What would Derek be like as a boyfriend? Controlling, possessive, challenging. Yes to all of the above.

She thought of the man she'd danced with on Saturday night. The humble, comforting Derek with the dry sense of humor. The one who'd held her hand and stroked her hair.

She'd barely scratched his surface. Did she want to?

Yes and no. Yes, because men like him were rare. She wanted to know what drove him, made him who he is. To have all that seething intensity focused on her...it would never be boring, that was for certain.

No, because the more she knew about him, the harder he would be to forget.

But Ginger knew one thing. She missed him so badly her chest ached. The thought of letting Derek go without at least making an attempt at something more left her feeling empty.

Tomorrow, she'd listen to what he had to say. Then she'd decide.

Where is that noise coming from?

She peeled her hands away from her sensitive eyes and spotted her cell phone buzzing and dancing on the coffee table she'd been working on prior to passing out. Her clock said 1:45 a.m. The screen of her cell displayed an unknown number with a Chicago area code. Who would be calling her at this time of night?

"Hello?"

"Oh, Ginger. Thank God. I've called three times."

She recognized the thick Chicago accent. Patty, the lady she'd met at the charity event. Something sank heavily in her stomach. No one called at this time of night with good news, and their only connection was Derek.

Stall. Put it off. "How...how did you get this number?"

"We exchanged numbers, don't you remember?"

She couldn't think past anything over the pounding in her head. "Oh. Okay."

"Listen dear, I don't know if this call is appropriate or not, but you and Derek seemed so close the other night. I thought you would want to know. There was a massive raid this evening at a meeting between two major gangs that resulted in some serious gunfire, and Derek has been taken to Saint Anthony's medical center. I just thought you'd want to know."

Ginger's body felt numb. "He's been shot?"

"Saint Anthony's. Fourteenth floor, ICU. I would get there as soon as possible."

The line went dead. Ginger couldn't make her body move for a full minute. Everything around her felt too clear. Every sound, even the feel of the carpet under her legs, felt abrasive, like a scrape along her nerve endings. She pushed herself up on shaking legs, stumbled into the bathroom, and stared at her reflection in the mirror under the harsh fluorescent light.

She'd barely finished brushing her teeth before her knees buckled and she landed on the tile floor. Pain came screaming through the numbness so swiftly, she doubled over with a cry. Eventually she found the strength to struggle to her feet. She stumbled back through the bedroom and out the apartment door, shoving her feet into her cowboy boots as she went.

Ginger got in her truck and drove aimlessly in one direction before realizing she didn't know Saint Anthony's location. At a stoplight, she begged for directions from an off-duty taxi driver, made a U-turn and finally headed the right way. Her drive to the hospital blurred together in a series of stoplights and street signs. Nothing felt real. Maybe she still lay passed out on her bedroom floor and this was one big, wine-induced nightmare. She squeezed the steering wheel, felt the solidity of it beneath her hands, rolled down the window, and breathed in the damp air. No way was she dreaming. That meant Derek could at that very moment be dying. Dead, even.

She'd just seen him hours earlier, solid and reassuring in the hallway of the building. They were supposed to talk tomorrow. He hadn't even given Ginger the courtesy of letting her know he was on his way to risk his stupid neck, dammit. Maybe she wouldn't have been so stubborn if she'd known.

Give me a chance, beautiful girl.

Hot, salty tears dripped from her eyes as she turned down the street leading to Saint Anthony's. Ginger could barely read the sign through her blurry vision, but somehow mustered the capability to park the truck and run inside. Bypassing the front desk, she headed straight for the elevators and punched the button for the fourteenth floor.

Ignoring the flower-toting family staring at her dishevelment with open curiosity, Ginger blinked through her tears at the numbers above the doors as they ticked away, moving so slowly she wanted to scream in frustration. When the doors finally parted, she took off like a shot, her eyes scanning the floor frantically. They finally landed on a desk with an official-looking woman sitting behind it, typing away on a computer.

She didn't bother wiping her eyes or trying to fix her appearance. None of it mattered.

"Excuse me. I'm here to see Derek Tyler. Lieutenant Derek Tyler. He's been shot. Please, I need to see him right away."

The redhead dressed in scrubs looked bored by Ginger's plea, taking her time looking up from the screen. "Spell the name."

Ginger bit back an exasperated groan. She needed to see Derek and this woman clearly didn't get the urgency. How many lieutenants had come in shot that night that she couldn't remember him? Jesus, had she even made it in time? How much time had passed since the phone call? It could have been minutes or hours for all she knew. "T-Y-L-E-R. As in, *Tyler*. Please, I need to see him."

Long fingernails punched the keyboard slowly. The woman shook her head. "No one has been admitted with that name, miss."

Ginger finally lost her patience along with any composure she'd managed to keep since entering the hospital. She got angry. And when she got angry, she cried. Hiccupping once, twice, sloppy tears began rolling down her face once more. She leaned over the desk until her face was inches from the redhead.

"Check again. *Now*. Or I'll throw this goddamn machine out the window."

"Ginger?"

Chapter Nineteen

Her heart stopped. Sagging back from the counter, away from the woman's stunned expression, Ginger turned to see Derek standing at the end of the corridor, underneath a sign that read WAITING ROOM.

With his ever-present badge clipped to his waist, Derek looked bone-weary, his white shirt wrinkled and speckled with blood. Stubble covered his wide jaw. He looked at her in shock as if he couldn't believe she stood there, just a short distance away. Her eyes ran over him, taking in every detail, never wanting to forget a single thing about him.

She sobbed. "Oh God. Oh, Derek."

Ginger's body shook so severely, she couldn't run to Derek as fast as she wanted to, but somehow made it to the end of the corridor. She leaped into his open arms, wrapped her body around him, and held on tight. His steady heartbeat drummed against her chest, reassuring her. With her face pressed into his strong shoulder, she wept harder than she could remember.

"Shhh, baby. I've got you. It's going to be okay. God,

you're frozen."

Derek hadn't been shot and killed. He was alive and vital, holding her in his arms where she belonged. Ginger repeated those facts over and over in her head. Or maybe she said them out loud. She couldn't be certain.

Slowly, she became aware of her surroundings. They stood in the center of a waiting room occupied by at least forty uniformed police officers and detectives. With her legs wrapped around his waist. Crying like a baby. Yelping, Ginger buried her face against his neck to block out all the amused grins.

Derek strode out of the waiting room and stopped in the first unoccupied hospital room they came across. Even after the door closed behind them, she could hear the whoops and catcalls echoing from the waiting room. Making no mention of the noise, he set her down on a narrow hospital bed, scanning her tearstained face.

"Sweetheart, talk to me. What's wrong? Did something happen to Willa?"

"No," she hiccupped, staring into his handsome, concerned face. "They told me someone shot you. They said I should get here as soon as possible."

"Me? No, one of my officers was wounded. We're just waiting for him to be moved into recovery." Derek looked dumbfounded. "*Who* called you?"

"Patty," she sniffed. "So you weren't shot? You're really okay?"

His jaw hardened. "I'm fine. Though I won't be able to say the same for Patty much longer."

"I don't understand."

Derek sighed. "Think about it. Did she actually say I'd been shot or did she just let you think it?"

She thought for a minute, paling at the realization. "Why would she do that to me?"

He made an irritated sound. "She must have guessed that based on my mood this morning, we'd broken up or had a fight. I'm guessing this was her misguided way of throwing us together."

Ginger brushed the final tears from her eyes. "Wow. That is a woman who takes matchmaking seriously. And here I thought she wanted to fix me up with her nephew."

"Over my dead body."

"It almost was."

Derek smiled, but it quickly disappeared. "How did you get here?"

She had to think. "Um…I drove my truck."

Eyes pinching shut, he took a steadying breath. "You drove yourself here, upset, in the middle of the night. Dressed in your pajamas."

Ginger glanced down, surprised to find herself in short terry-cloth shorts, a nightshirt and cowboy boots. "Huh. Look at that." Gazing into his green eyes once more, she stroked his jaw until it relaxed a little. "I wasn't thinking straight, I suppose."

Derek still looked displeased.

Her hands moved to his chest, stroking over his shoulders. "So I've made my big, dramatic scene. Isn't this the part where you kiss me, Lieutenant?"

"I can't kiss you right now."

"Why not?"

His chest rose and fell with a shudder underneath her hands. "I'm looking at you sitting there all puffy-eyed from crying over me. If I kiss you right now, I'll never stop."

Her heart pounded a wild beat. "Just one little kiss?"

Derek groaned. "God, this is how it's going to be with you, isn't it? When I can't make love to you properly, you'll beg me for it? I think you're trying to kill me."

Smiling, Ginger ran her nose along the side of his neck.

"I need you alive for what I have in mind."

His head dropped forward. "Being shot would have been easier than this."

Ginger jerked back with a gasp, her eyes going wide. "Don't say that."

"I'm sorry." Derek grabbed her wrists and blocked her with his hips before she could slide off the bed and get away from him. "Bad joke." When a tear slipped out, Derek watched it track down her cheek.

With a soft groan, he kissed her, tenderly at first. She let her head fall back, parting her lips underneath his, granting permission.

Ginger whimpered and molded her body against his harder, muscular frame. Derek's hands were everywhere, running up her bare calves and thighs, whipping off her nightshirt to reveal her naked breasts, then cupping and kneading them greedily. He gripped her knees and yanked her forward to the edge of the bed so he could rock into her body, despite their remaining clothes.

"If you keep quiet, I'll give you what you need. Can you do that?" He drove his demanding erection forward between her legs, and Ginger's eyes rolled back in her head.

"*Yes.*"

"But you're going to give me what I need first, Ginger. Do you remember what you said to me the other night? I do. Every fucking word." His mouth found her breast, drawing a nipple between his lips and sucking hard. Ginger bit her lip but a moan of longing escaped, echoing through the room.

"I told you to keep *quiet*. If you don't listen to me, we can't do this."

Her hands clutched at his hair as he tongued her nipples. "I'll be quiet, I swear," she whispered.

"If even *one* of my men hears your sweet little noises when you come, I'll be very upset. Those are for my ears alone. Do you understand me?"

"Yes. Yes, I understand."

"Good." He rewarded her with a slow, provocative kiss of her mouth. "You asked me if I wanted to put it in your mouth. You asked if I wanted to be your first again."

She watched through hooded eyes as his hands worked the buckle of his belt. Then he reached behind him to flip the lock on the door, his savage gaze not leaving hers for a second. Ginger felt drugged, but completely focused at the same time. She desperately wanted to please Derek and didn't care if that made her weak-willed, because she planned on demanding he please her just as thoroughly afterward. Her body shook and heated under his regard to such a degree, she almost climaxed then and there.

Derek took Ginger's hand, placing it against the stiff bulge behind his fly, and pressed his hips forward suggestively. "I haven't been the same since you said those things to me. I've been in a bad way, baby."

Unable to wait any longer, Ginger unzipped his pants and dropped to her knees. She took his hands and placed them on either side of her head. "Show me what you want."

"There's nothing you can do that I won't love."

Gripping the thick base in her hand, she didn't allow herself to think, just followed her instincts. She tasted every inch of him with her tongue, lips, and teeth, listening to his increased breathing or growls to judge what he liked. His fists wrapped themselves in her hair, indicating when to speed up or slow down. She couldn't get enough of his taste, the sounds of pleasure he made. When Derek tried to pull her away, Ginger didn't want to stop and told him so.

"Trust me, I don't want you to stop either, baby. But I need to feel you come." He gripped her by the shoulders and pulled her to her feet, kissing and licking at her mouth until her body undulated against his once more. "Dammit, I swore the next time I had you, I would go slowly."

She tore her mouth away, panting. "No. I don't want you to hold back. Take me however you want me."

Before she could finish voicing her appeal, Derek spun her around until she faced away from him. She flattened her hands on the high bed to balance herself as he crouched down low behind her and peeled the shorts from her legs. Absently, she registered the rip of a condom wrapper and the faint sound of Derek rolling it onto his erection.

After he'd finished seeing to their protection, Ginger's short puffs of breath were the only sound to be heard in the room, until Derek finally spoke.

"No panties again, sweetheart?" He made a guttural noise of either approval or disapproval. She couldn't tell without seeing his face. "If I didn't think the sound of my palm against your ass would draw attention, I would remind you how much your forgetfulness pleases me." Ginger's sharp inhalations accelerated even more, her chest heaving. "I'll have to show you a different way, I suppose."

Then he bit her. His teeth sank into the flesh of her ass, stopping just before they broke the skin. She didn't dare cry out, instead trapping the scream inside her throat. Before Ginger could truly register what he'd done, she heard his pants hit the floor, belt still attached. One arm snaked around her waist and held her steady as he thrust home inside her.

She couldn't prevent the hiss of pleasure from escaping through her teeth. The difference compared to last time astounded her. No pain, only fullness and the immediate urge to move.

Derek's chest pressed against her back, his hips tilting upward into hers so high and deep, the position forced Ginger onto her tiptoes. Then he pulled out, almost leaving her completely, before thrusting deep once more. Ginger bit her lip to keep from crying out, positive she drew blood.

"Do you feel that, baby? That's your man moving inside you."

Bracing herself on her elbows, she ground back against him, circling her hips and begging him to keep moving, but he seemed determined to set the pace.

"*Please*, Derek."

He thrust hard and quick exactly five times, just enough for Ginger to get used to the rhythm before slowing once more. "Who's fucking you, Ginger?"

She knew what he wanted to hear. Throwing her head back, she reveled in every word. "My man. My man is fucking me."

With a stifled growl, he yanked her back against him and pumped his hips up and into her wildly. Ginger held on to the bed, absorbing each thrust that carried her closer to release.

"*Fuck*, baby. I'll never get used to how tight you are."

Derek's hand slid over her hip and found her clitoris, applying pressure and friction with his middle finger until Ginger's body shuddered and shook with the most powerful orgasm she'd ever experienced. A minute later, Derek followed, groaning his release into the side of her neck.

When their breathing returned to normal, Derek kissed Ginger's shoulder and pulled out of her slowly. Then he turned her in his arms so he could hold her.

"I can't seem to control myself long enough to show you we're not just about sex." She felt him shake his head. "Even so, Ginger, I'm not going to apologize for what just happened. When we touch each other, it's honest and real. I crave it."

Ginger remained silent, absorbing Derek's warmth. She wanted to forget the agony of the last hour and simply enjoy being held, but she couldn't. The uncertainty of what lay ahead for them didn't scare her nearly as much as losing him. She'd learned that hard lesson tonight.

"I know that now." Sucking in a shaky breath, she gave

him her honesty. "When I thought you'd been shot, maybe even before that, I realized you were right. What I feel for you…it's not only physical."

Arms tightening around her, he started to speak, but she laid a hand on his chest to stop him. She'd just taken a big step admitting her feelings and needed to let it settle.

"I know sex doesn't define us, Derek. But maybe it's an important part of what's between us. And I think that's okay. We're people who need more than words. Can we agree on that?"

Derek kissed the top of her head, holding her close. "You won't get any argument from me." He tilted her chin so he could meet her eyes. "But someday, when we need reassurance from each other, our words will be enough. I promise, Ginger."

Chapter Twenty

After a hot shower, Derek collapsed into bed around 7:00 a.m. His body felt sore from the overwhelming tension of the day and needed sleep to repair itself. Despite his exhaustion, he couldn't deny the unfamiliar sense of contentment he felt. Last night, after buying Ginger a cup of coffee at the hospital to keep her awake, he'd given her his jacket and walked her to the parking lot. She'd refused to let him call her a cab, so he'd settled for her promise to text him when she arrived at home.

It came twenty minutes later: *Home sugar xo.*

He'd caught Alvarez eyeing him funny in the waiting room and realized he was smiling like a kid on Christmas. Highly inappropriate behavior when a man lay wounded in the next room. Even if they knew for certain he would pull through. Sensing the room full of officers was dying to know more about the gorgeous, half-dressed girl who'd jumped him in the hallway, he'd silenced the first one brave enough to ask with a look that prevented any more questions.

Before she left the hospital, he'd extricated one more promise from her. When Willa left for school this morning,

Derek wanted her to come over. He still planned on having their talk despite what took place last night. He'd clipped his spare keys back on her key ring so she wouldn't have an excuse not to come.

Just before he let sleep overcome him, Derek recalled Ginger standing in the hospital, shaking from the cold in her nightshirt, crying because she'd thought him dead or dying. He'd never had anyone cry or worry over him before. Both of his parents were accountants living downstate who didn't understand his chosen profession and distanced themselves from the chaos of it, of his life.

Women he'd dated in the past seemed to enjoy his dangerous job, even get off on it. Or they would venture in the opposite direction and suggest he quit *because* of the danger. Ginger would want him safe, but she would never ask him to change his lifestyle or give up the job he loved. Since meeting her, he'd been irrationally jealous, dominated her sexually, and provoked her at every turn. Yet, she'd run toward him and jumped straight in his arms this morning, wanting him flaws and all.

Derek hoped for her sake she didn't try to change her mind, because he didn't intend to let her go. He would fight every single insecurity swimming around in that beautiful head to keep her. Hell, he had insecurities, too. Could he make a woman like Ginger happy outside of bed? He'd spent thirty years remaining emotionally detached from the opposite sex, but if he was going to demand Ginger open up and trust him, he couldn't keep her at a distance. Nor did he want to.

Despite the troubling details he'd discovered about her past, he still needed to learn so much about her. In addition to her loyalty to Willa, he knew her to be strong-willed and perceptive, funny and compassionate. She'd been ruthless about taking a different path than her mother, but still used her looks to make men hop when she needed something. A fact that set him on edge. He alone would see to her needs now.

He felt her slip into bed with him at eight thirty. Waiting to see what she would do, Derek kept his breathing even and remained still. The mattress barely moved under her slight weight, but he felt her lift the covers and scoot across the bed, closer to him. After a moment wherein he struggled against rolling over and pinning her, Ginger's arm slid around his waist and she pressed herself against him.

Powerful relief moved through him. Derek realized he hadn't fully expected her to feel the same way in the light of day. Knowing that she hadn't changed her mind about giving them a chance calmed him immeasurably. He lay there, letting her feminine scent wrap around him, relishing his body's response to having her in his bed.

"I know you're awake," she whispered against his ear, making him smile. "I shared a room with my sister for seventeen years. I know when someone's being a big faker.

"Guilty. I think I'm afraid to turn around and see what you look like in my bed. The image will haunt me when I leave for work this afternoon."

Her laugh sounded muffled among the pillows. "But if you don't turn around, you won't see the sexy lingerie I wore just for you."

Derek flipped over with such speed, Ginger squealed and threw up her hands. Kneeling over her, he yanked down the covers and narrowed his eyes at her oversize sweatshirt and leggings. "Oh, you'll pay for that."

Her smile slipped a little. "I've just been so cold since last night. It's like I can't warm up."

He'd been right to avoid looking at her. Seeing Ginger snuggled in his bed, so casually dressed with her hair fanning out onto his pillow, Derek's heart wedged itself in his throat.

She had to be the most goddamn beautiful thing on the planet, even sleep-deprived as she appeared.

"Come here. Let's get you warm."

He lay back down alongside Ginger, sliding an arm underneath her so she could rest her head on his shoulder. She hesitated only a moment before tucking her head under his chin and cuddling into the warmth of his bare chest.

"Is the wounded officer okay?"

"Yes, moved out of ICU around four-thirty this morning."

"Good." She blew out a breath. "I guess I made kind of a scene."

Derek sighed. "I don't think any of them particularly minded the interruption. While we're on the subject, could you try and pay a little closer attention to your attire in public? I'd barely recovered from those firemen seeing you in that wet T-shirt the night your apartment flooded. Now the entire homicide division knows what you wear to bed."

"Actually, I don't wear anything to bed. I fell asleep last night before I could get undressed." Ginger laughed when Derek groaned, pulling her tighter against him. "How can you be so jealous of other men, Derek, when you know there's only been you?"

"Baby, I'm jealous of men who haven't even seen you yet."

She smirked. "I could tell you there's nothing to worry about, but I think I'd be wasting my breath."

"Tell me anyway."

Leaning up to kiss his lips gently, Ginger obeyed, whispered the reassurance to him twice. When she tried to deepen the kiss, Derek pulled back.

"Don't try to distract me. We have too much to discuss. Including why you were so dressed up yesterday afternoon."

Ginger flopped back onto the pillow. "Oh, that." He held on to his impatience while she fidgeted with the bedspread nervously. "I had lunch with a man who owns a furniture store in Wicker Park. I bought some antique chairs there last week and we got to talking about my designs. He asked to see pictures, so we met for lunch and I showed him some."

"And?"

"And he wants to sell them in his shop."

She still wouldn't look at him, so he grasped her chin and turned her until their eyes met. "Ginger, that's great. You weren't going to say anything?"

"Not unless they sold."

"They'll sell," he said with confidence.

"Well, let's hope so. I called Sensation yesterday and quit."

He tried to keep the sweeping relief from his face. "You're full of surprises this morning. Is there a particular reason?"

She ran the arch of her foot along his calf. "Besides my boyfriend showing up and raising hell? Dragging me out in the middle of my shift?"

"Say that again."

"Which part?"

"The part where you call me your boyfriend with that accent that makes me crazy."

"I'll say it again if you kiss me."

He smiled and shook his head. "All in good time, sweetheart."

"If you insist," she sighed. "But if this is going to be a long conversation, I'm going to get comfortable."

She grabbed the hem of her sweatshirt and peeled it over her head to reveal a cropped pink tank top that bared just a hint of her smooth stomach. Then she stretched out like a cat right in front of him.

Derek's fingers dug into the comforter to prevent himself from reaching for her. He'd sworn to himself they would talk this morning. Ginger counted on sex as a means to distract him. And, God, watching her slide around on his sheets, he came damn close to forgetting his resolve. But if he gave in every time, they would never move forward. She probably didn't even realize the extent to which she used her sensuality to avoid having difficult conversations.

Last night had been a turning point, but despite the progress they'd made at the hospital, he'd need to walk a fine line with Ginger. He needed her trust.

Derek dragged his gaze away from her body. "Tell me why you really quit."

Her eyes shot to his in surprise, then glanced away. "Honestly? I'd called security ten minutes earlier about that guy who grabbed me. They didn't take me seriously. If you hadn't shown up…" she trailed off, oblivious to his mounting anger. "You don't know a lot about where I came from. I worked in a place called Bobby's Hideaway for four years before I left Nashville. The kind of thing you saw that night happened frequently there. When I left Nashville, I left that behind. I don't want to feel unsafe at my job anymore."

Fury gripped him by the neck. For the girl she'd been and the woman she'd become. He'd die before he let her go through anything resembling her past life again.

His voice shook. "You don't ever have to feel unsafe again. I won't allow it."

Apprehension clouded her features. "I made a decision on the drive home last night from the hospital. If we're really going to try this…"

"We are."

Her eyes squeezed shut. "Then there are some things I want you to know about me first. Things you deserve to know."

Chapter Twenty-One

Ginger's heart pounded. She was actually going to tell Derek about the money she'd stolen. Everything that happened next between them would depend on his reaction. She didn't harbor any fears that he would arrest her or demand she return the cash to Valerie. She could rest easy on that score. But one thing she'd learned about Derek? He took his job as a law officer very seriously. How would he feel about having a thief in his bed?

If anyone had told her a week ago she would be considering a relationship, with a *cop* no less, she would have laughed and called that person a filthy liar. Well, here she was. And she'd be damned if she'd waste her time pretending to be someone else. He would accept the worst of her or nothing at all.

Maybe she'd shed a little bit of her former self this week by quitting Sensation and taking a meeting with an actual businessman about her furniture. But she would never completely shed the girl from Nashville who'd once flashed her breasts at a hardware store owner in exchange for him installing a deadbolt on her and Willa's bedroom door. *That*

Ginger had worked with what the good Lord gave her, and she would never be ashamed of her actions.

Only one question remained. Would Derek be ashamed of her?

"Willa and I didn't have the best of upbringings," she started, hating her voice for shaking. "Our mother, Valerie, she had me young and...she wasn't quite ready for a kid. And by the time Willa came along, she still wasn't ready." She took a deep breath. "I've had to do things maybe some people wouldn't approve of to keep us clothed and fed—"

"Ginger, I know."

Her expression went from anxious to confused. "You know what exactly?"

Derek released a breath and placed a hand on her arm, like maybe he thought once he explained, she would make a run for it. Unease spread through her.

"Please try not to get upset."

She didn't say anything.

He sighed. "I ran a search of your name on the national database. There was a missing persons report filed for you and Willa, by your mother, three weeks ago."

Ginger couldn't get air into her lungs. She lurched up in the bed, hand clutching her chest, vaguely sensing the alarm in Derek's voice. Valerie had gone to the police and reported them missing. That could only mean one of two things. Their mother had suddenly decided she gave a damn—highly unlikely considering the condition she'd been in when Ginger last saw her—or something was very wrong. Her mother didn't associate with cops unless they were in the process of arresting her. If she'd walked into a police station without handcuffs on her wrists, there must be a damn good reason.

The money. Ginger never really stopped to ponder where it might have come from. Derek said Valerie filed a missing persons report, but hadn't mentioned the theft. Which meant

Valerie needed to find Ginger to get the money back.

But she would never involve the cops unless her circumstances were dire. Life or death. Either it hadn't been her money to begin with and she'd been holding it for someone who now needed it back. Or she'd borrowed the cash and her debt was coming due.

How could Ginger not have seen this coming? Besides the police, who else was looking for them? And how could Derek have brought her into a room full of cops knowing about the missing persons report?

Ginger threw her legs over the side of the bed, intending to go pick up Willa from school. She couldn't think beyond that. She just knew she didn't want her little sister out there alone.

Derek pushed her back down onto the bed, looming above her.

"Get off me!"

"Jesus, will you just *listen* to me?"

She fought him, but his hips pinned her to the bed. "No. Let me up!"

"I took care of it! Ginger, I took care of it."

Her body went still underneath him. "What does that mean?"

"It *means* no one will be looking for you in Chicago. There's no way to delete the report, but I found a way to hide it. When I said you didn't have to feel unsafe anymore, I meant it." His eyes searched wildly around the room. "Dammit, Ginger. Where the hell were you going? Were you going to leave me? Leave town?"

Relief warred with the adrenaline still pulsing through her. "I don't know. I don't know! What was I supposed to do? Every cop at that event, the ones in the hospital…they've all seen me, know my name. Willa is a minor. What I did is considered kidnapping."

"Don't ever try to leave without hearing me out first, okay?"

The panic on Derek's face broke through her racing thoughts. Whether or not she approved of his checking into her background, ultimately he'd compromised himself for her. Should she be grateful or furious? She didn't know. Nothing seemed clear anymore. But she needed time to figure it out. Her plan to tell Derek about the stolen money could wait for another day.

"So you know my mother's name now. You must have seen her rap sheet."

"Yes," he confirmed in a hushed voice.

"I guess you know all about me then. I had this big confession ready and you already knew."

"There's nothing in your past that could keep me away from you." Derek's voice radiated sincerity. "You can tell me anything."

Ginger struggled against the tears gathering behind her eyes. Derek scrutinized her expression, as if he knew she held something back, but he didn't press.

The barrier she'd erected between them had never truly existed. While she'd been pretending to be carefree, no-strings-attached Ginger, he'd known about the past weighing her down. It made her angry. It made her want to blot out the knowledge she saw in his eyes.

Ginger became aware of their position on the bed, his body wedged between her parted thighs. His obvious arousal told her he hadn't remained unaffected. Ginger's arms were pinned over her head, bringing their chests and stomachs flush. She could see the battle taking place on his face. Sympathy warred with his need for her.

"Don't look at me like that," she snapped.

"Like what?"

"Like you feel sorry for me."

"How do you want me to look at you, Ginger?"

She locked her ankles behind his back, watched him shudder. "Look at me like you did last night."

With a loud groan of surrender, she felt the remaining anxiety in his body melt away, replaced by a different kind of tension. Derek rocked against her, claiming her mouth and biting at her lips until she offered her tongue. Liquid heat poured through her, spreading and warming everything in its path. Within seconds, her body craved him to the point of pain.

Ginger tugged her hands from his grip above her head. When they broke for air, she ripped her shirt off over her head and watched his eyes go dark as she molded her own breasts in her palms, tugging her nipples between her thumb and finger.

"Oh, baby, yes. Play with your tits for me. Show me where you want my mouth."

Her thumbs caressed circles around her nipples. "Here, Derek."

A heartbeat later, his mouth descended onto her breast, flicking the pink bud with his tongue before drawing the tightened tip into his mouth. Ginger's head tossed on the pillow as he went back and forth between her breasts, rolling the stiff peaks in circles under his palms, blowing against them softly and grazing them with his teeth until she cried out for him to stop.

He raised his head, dark green eyes still riveted on her reddened, glistening nipples. "Where do you want me next, Ginger?"

The deep resonance of his voice washed over her, making her body tremble. Bravely, she took one hand and trailed it down her bare stomach, watching his diligent mouth follow in its wake, kissing and nipping at the sensitive skin of her belly. Finally, her fingers dipped below the waistband of her leggings, signaling where she wanted him to go. He caught her hand before it went too far, biting her sensitive palm in reproof.

"You like my tongue between your thighs, don't you, sweetheart?" He hooked his thumbs into her waistband and slowly began sliding the leggings down her legs, along with her black thong. Ginger's hips writhed in response to his question. "Yes, I know you do. I still have the nail marks on my shoulders from last time to prove it."

Derek knelt at the end of the bed and slid his big hands underneath her ass. He gripped her tightly, urging her legs over his shoulders. Ginger's body quaked in anticipation of his mouth finding her most sensitive place. She reached above her head and curled her fingers around the headboard for leverage.

Derek took his time looking her over before nipping at her inner thigh.

"Please, Derek," she whimpered.

He smiled wickedly. "Can I tell you a dirty secret?"

"Yes," she gasped. "Just hurry."

Derek's dark laughter increased her arousal, coating her in slick heat. Achingly slow, he sunk two thick fingers inside her. "If I could go back and do one thing differently that first night, I would taste your virgin pussy before I fucked you. I bet it would have been extra sweet."

Ginger climaxed. Her scream resonated through the room, ending in disjointed pants and moans as Derek prolonged the pleasure with his fingers. Arching away from the bed, she rotated her hips against his hand, never wanting the rippling spasms to end.

When she finally opened her eyes, Ginger sought his face and found him watching her with reverence. "God, you're incredible." Then his mouth found her core once more, licking the sensitive flesh with long, torturous strokes of his tongue, focusing on and exploiting the bundle of nerves begging for attention. Digging her fingers into his broad shoulders, she hurtled toward a second peak.

Derek growled as she came again, this time against his mouth. Ginger heard the now-familiar sound of him ripping open a condom wrapper with his teeth.

"I take it back. Nothing could taste sweeter than that."

He jerked her hips up to rest on his thighs, pushed her legs wide, and filled her with his erection. As vulnerable and exposed as the position left her, Ginger had no choice but to match his demanding rhythm.

She needed his full weight on top of her, though, pressing her down into the mattress. She wanted to feel mastered, overcome. "I need you on top of me now. Please. I need…you to hold me down."

His sharp eyes focused on her. "Baby, do you know what hearing that does to me?"

Following her down onto the bed, he pinned her soft body with his harder one, without sacrificing one precious movement of his body inside hers. Ginger sobbed at the perfection of it.

"Tighten those pretty thighs around my waist. I'm going to give it to you rough." She obeyed. Holding her arms near the headboard, immobilizing her, Derek pounded into her. The sound of damp, slapping flesh and the metal headboard bumping against the wall echoed through the room, mingling with Ginger's cries and Derek's sharp expletives. "Is this how you wanted it, beautiful girl?"

"Oh God, yes. Harder, Derek."

She didn't think it possible, but he complied with her plea, pushing the headboard against the wall with even greater force. Ginger felt her body reaching for another orgasm and raced to meet it. Her wrists ached from being held in his punishing grip, but the pain of restraint only heightened her experience. She tugged on the unyielding hands holding her hostage and felt the dizzying heat move through her lower abdomen when she couldn't get free.

"Derek!"

"I'm here, baby."

The orgasm shook through Ginger. Derek thrust deep and ground his pelvis against her. Her insides quaked while her body remained completely restricted, unable to move. Ironically, she'd never felt freer in her life. The room dimmed and spun around her as she tried to hold on to the sensation, to memorize it.

Ginger knew eventually she'd have to question why being restrained fulfilled her and how Derek sensed it and indulged her needs so perfectly, but right now she could only focus on keeping her legs locked around Derek's back as drove into her one final time and peaked.

"Ginger. Baby. *Ginger!*"

His grasp loosened as he climaxed, and she used the freedom to grab his ass and pull him deep. Sinking his teeth into her shoulder, he groaned. Ginger wrapped her arms around him when he finally collapsed, placing kisses along his collarbone and neck.

Rolling onto his side a while later, Derek pulled her hard against his chest. He didn't speak, instead seeming content to watch her. One hand stroked her hair, separating the sweaty strands from her neck and face.

His continued silence began to unnerve her. Derek had called all the shots every time they'd been together. Maybe she'd made him uncomfortable, asking him to hold her down?

She kept her head on his chest, mortified over her brazenness. "I'm sorry."

The hand stroking her hair stilled, and she held her breath. "Why?"

"You're so quiet." She paused to gather her courage. "I

figured what I asked you to do...was it... not normal? Or wrong?"

She squeaked as Derek flipped her over onto her back. When she looked up into his face, it was covered in disbelief. "Ginger, you listen to me very carefully. *Nothing* we do together is wrong. *Ever.*" He shook his head. "If I'm quiet it's because I'm trying to figure out a way to never leave this bed again. That was—"

She didn't let him finish. Relief roared through her, and with a laugh, she sat up, threw her arms around his neck, and hugged him. At first, Derek seemed stunned by her action. But his arms slowly banded around her waist and held her so tight she struggled to breathe.

"You have no idea how happy hearing that makes me, Lieutenant."

His laugh rumbled against her ear. Without breaking their embrace, he pulled her back down onto the bed, tucking her head into his neck. "Me, too. Sleep, now, beautiful girl. I don't have to be at work for a few hours."

Ginger snuggled in close. Within minutes, she started drifting off, lulled by the fingers stroking up and down her spine.

Chapter Twenty-Two

"Hot damn, Wip. We've got a stone-cold fox on our hands."

Willa flipped Ginger the bird without looking away from the full-length mirror. "This touching family sitcom moment brought to you by the letters F and U."

Her sister tried valiantly to play down the transformation she'd undergone in the last hour, but Ginger noticed the flush of pleasure on her cheeks as she surveyed her appearance.

They stood in Ginger's bedroom early Saturday evening getting Willa dressed for prom. Something Ginger never would have believed a month ago. She'd found the heather gray cocktail dress Willa now wore at a vintage shop in Noble Square after hunting for half a day. Sensing Willa would balk at anything too colorful, she'd didn't mind congratulating herself on picking the simple, strapless dress that fit Willa's small frame to perfection.

Willa gave Ginger full creative control, and after removing the heavy black eyeliner, Ginger had applied a tasteful amount of makeup, playing up her sister's natural glow, and pulled her hair away from her face in a classic twist.

If Ginger hadn't shared a room with Willa for seventeen years, she would barely recognize her except for the nose ring.

"What time is Evan coming to pick you up?"

"Seven-thirty. We're going to dinner with some of his friends before the dance."

Ginger nodded, trying to appear as confident as Willa. This is where they differed. Ginger thrived in social situations where she didn't have to interact with one single person. She could jump from conversation to conversation and move on when the subject got too heavy or personal. Willa, on the other hand, didn't generally play well with others. Not that Ginger didn't have faith in her sister, especially this new, school-activity-participating Willa. But she knew she'd worry until Willa walked through the door later.

Ginger produced a black sequined clutch that she'd kept hidden in her closet and handed it to Willa. As she'd predicted, it looked fabulous with the dress and matching black heels.

Their eyes met in the mirror. "Please make sure you take your cell phone, Willa. There is some money in the purse if you need it. For dinner. For a cab. Anything."

Willa laughed at Ginger's fierce expression, then sobered. "Ginger, I'm going to be fine. It just seems like a big deal because I never go out."

"Okay, just a few more things and I'll be finished." She took a deep breath. "No drugs. No getting into a car with someone who has been drinking. Don't have sex on the first date, but if you do, there's a condom in the purse. Please, please don't need to use it. But I won't ask if you did."

"Oh, my God."

"Shut up. You look beautiful. Have a great time."

Willa's face broke into a dazzling smile. "Thanks for the dress, the makeup. Everything."

Ginger held back her tears. "You're welcome."

Her sister looked like she wanted to say something else but hesitated.

"Spit it out, Wip."

"Am I being a jackass, trusting Evan like this?"

Ginger thought for a moment, taking the question seriously. It might have been posed in typical Willa fashion, but vulnerability lingered behind it. "No, you're not being a jackass. Is it a risk? Yes. But I don't think you'd place your trust easily, Willa. Now you just have to have faith in your own judgment. Coming to Chicago was a risk, but we took it. Maybe it's time we take a few more."

Willa nodded, absorbing her words. "Kind of like you with the lieutenant?"

At the mention of Derek, Ginger felt her insides melt. He'd been working around the clock since the raid, busy with paperwork and interrogations of the arrested men. She'd woken alone in Derek's bed in the early evening after their morning together. Disoriented at having slept through most of the day, she'd stretched her tender muscles and risen to return to her own apartment, trying her best not to panic over his having left a second time without saying good-bye.

On the counter in Derek's kitchen, she'd found a white sack of chocolate doughnuts and a carton of orange juice, sitting on top of a giant stack of magazines. Smiling cautiously, she'd ripped off the note attached to the bag with her name written on it.

Make me something. I want a reminder of you in my apartment at all times.

Of course he couldn't just buy her flowers. That wouldn't have been his style. Knowing the perfect piece to use, she'd retrieved it from her apartment and spent the rest of the evening in Derek's place, munching on doughnuts and working on his project. And okay, maybe she'd snooped a little in the name of inspiration. He didn't keep photographs around the apartment, which made her wonder about his family. In the kitchen cabinet, she'd found a shoebox full of Cubs baseball cards ruthlessly sorted by date, and an envelope tucked inside containing ticket stubs dating back to the eighties.

Her little discoveries, including his collection of old Western movies, made Ginger grow more and more curious about him and how he'd grown up. Had she been so focused on hiding her past from him, she'd overlooked the fact that he hid one, too?

Although his schedule hadn't permitted time for any more meaningful conversations, he called and texted her throughout his workday, clearly making a concerted effort to assuage her fears.

The content of those text and phone exchanges often made her blush.

Yesterday, her phone beeped while in the produce aisle of the supermarket. Checking the screen, she'd dropped a cantaloupe upon viewing the text message from Derek.

Craving you, Ginger.

She could have texted him back that she'd thought of him constantly since their morning in bed. Or how needing him had become a constant physical ache. But she wanted to say those things to him in person, so she'd replied:

Oooh. I have two, ripe melons in my hands. Wanna see?

YES

She'd snapped a picture of the cantaloupes, sent it, and continued her shopping, chuckling to herself all the way through the frozen foods section.

That night, long after falling asleep, she'd woken to his hands stroking over her body. Up her legs, over her hips, circling her breasts, then down to caress between her thighs. Ginger always slept on her side and his naked body spooned her, back to front.

"Wake up, you little cock tease," he'd growled against her neck. Then he'd pushed into her from behind, taking her as she moaned into the pillow.

Ginger pulled herself out of the reveries and refocused on Willa. "Yes, like me and the lieutenant."

Her sister snorted. "Ginger, don't ever play poker for money."

Ten minutes later, a knock sounded at the door. Ginger made a shooing gesture to Willa, who stood in the kitchen. "Go in the other room. You have to make an entrance." Willa rolled her eyes but did as she was told. Ginger checked through the peephole to make sure Evan stood on the other side, then pulled open the door.

"Hey, Ginger."

"Evan." She stepped aside to let him in, hiding her smile over how handsome he looked in his black dress pants and button-down shirt. Her sister knew how to pick 'em. "Are you driving tonight?"

"No. My friends and I chipped in on a limo. I hope that's okay."

"As long as you don't use it as an excuse to drink. I don't care what you do on your own time, but I want my sister brought home safe, Mr. Carmichael."

Evan ran a nervous hand through his hair, messing it up further. "I'm not going to lie to you—some of my friends will probably drink tonight. But you have my word that I won't touch a drop. I want Willa safe, too."

She appreciated his honesty and smiled to let him know. "Okay, then. We understand each other."

"Ginger, can I come out now?" Willa called impatiently from her bedroom.

"I suppose."

The bedroom door opened and Ginger snapped Evan's reaction shot on her cell phone. He looked like he'd been struck dumb at the sight of Willa coming toward him. She saved the photo of Evan with the intention of showing it to Willa the next time she felt unsure of his feelings for her. The poor kid looked two seconds away from throwing himself at her feet.

"Whoa."

"Hey." Willa shifted from side to side, looking uneasy under Evan's scrutiny. She pretended to adjust the bracelet Ginger lent her to avoid his eyes.

"Willa, stop."

Both sisters gaped at Evan.

"Stop what?" Willa managed.

"I can tell you're freaking out." He held out his hand to her. "Stop."

Ginger watched, fascinated, as Willa's eyes glassed over and she bit her bottom lip. Nodding, she reached out and took his hand.

"You look beautiful," he breathed.

Willa's face transformed with her smile. Safely tucked into Evan's side, they walked to the door. Ginger stood rooted to her spot, unable to believe the exchange she'd just witnessed. How had Evan come to understand Willa so well in such a short period of time?

Letting Willa live her own life without interference had always seemed like the best approach, but now Ginger wasn't so sure. Of course, she provided support whenever necessary and she liked to think they were best friends. But maybe she'd chosen to remain at a distance because it was easier for her, not Willa. By ignoring their mutual past and making light of the horrors they'd experienced, she'd set a horrible example. *Pretend your problems don't exist and push through* had always been her philosophy. She never stopped to think it might be the wrong one. Willa had been given no choice but to follow suit.

It was time she fixed the mess she'd made.

Before they could walk out the door, Ginger stopped the couple. "Wait up, Wip. Evan, can I just have one minute with my sister?"

"Sure." He walked out into the hallway to wait, throwing one more glance at her over his shoulder as he went.

Willa searched her face. "What's up?"

Ginger fought to maintain her composure so as not to alarm Willa. She needed to find the right words to express her regret without giving herself away entirely.

"I just need to tell you that I'm going to do better. Okay? I want you to be as proud of me as I am of you right now. I'm going to do the right thing from now on."

Smiling, Willa shook her head. "Ginger, you're just emotional because I'm wearing a dress."

"You're right. That must be it," she lied.

"I promise I'll be back in a hoodie by tomorrow."

"Okay." Ginger opened the door and pushed her out. "Have fun, you two."

Ginger closed the door behind them and blew out a shaky breath. Then she turned and walked to the Dolly statue. With a small twist to the right, the blonde's head dislodged. She reached inside and pulled out the canvas bag.

Chapter Twenty-Three

Derek walked into his apartment and flipped on the lights. He set down the bottle of wine he'd picked up on the drive home and unstrapped his shoulder holster, laying it on the kitchen table. After finally wrapping up the paperwork and briefings pertaining to the Modesto case, he looked forward to a couple of much-needed days off. As soon as he took a shower and changed out of his wrinkled work clothes, he planned on dragging Ginger out of her apartment and into his bed. He'd see to her pleasure and then he'd damn well sleep for at least ten straight hours.

Tomorrow night, when he felt semi-human, he planned on taking Ginger out on an actual date. She'd been patient with his demanding work schedule. Almost too patient, as if she didn't expect anything from him. That shit would come to an end this weekend. He wanted Ginger to expect *everything* from him.

Derek refused to put off their conversation about the stolen money any longer. She'd been on the verge of telling him as they'd lain in bed together a few days ago, he was sure of it, but she'd balked at the last minute. Although he'd wanted to push, she'd already looked so damn vulnerable after his confession that he'd researched her past, Derek didn't have the heart. This weekend, he would come clean that he already knew. And there would no longer be any secrets between them. He wouldn't allow it to fester. Not when she meant so much to him.

Additionally, Derek hated having the loose end. So he'd tied it up. As long as Ginger remained in possession of the money, her safety would be in question. It made him crazed to think what could happen if a shady character such as Haywood Devon learned of her whereabouts. But with the help of his contact in Nashville and the national criminal database, Derek had found something he could use to put Devon behind bars for a long time, if not for good.

It had been his experience that, in most criminal enterprises, members tended to branch out when the well dried up. Which is exactly what happened a few years back for Devon when his then-partner left Nashville in search of greener pastures.

Thankfully, the partner in question had branched out to Chicago, bringing a wealth of information about his shady Nashville past, including valuable dirt on Devon. All Derek had to do was make him talk—something he planned to get right on now that they'd busted up Modesto's gang ring.

Derek caught Ginger's scent and turned, half expecting to find her waiting for him. Instead, he saw a lacquered box, decorated with one of Ginger's trademark designs, complete with a metal fastening where he could insert a lock. A gun box. Picking it up, he laughed at some of the magazine and newspaper headlines she'd interspersed with pictures of Dirty Harry and John Wayne.

DIRTY MOUTH? CLEAN IT UP!
GUNS DON'T KILL PEOPLE, ZOMBIES KILL PEOPLE.

MEAN PEOPLE DUCK.

Opening the lid, Derek found a note with his name on it, next to a smiley face. Positive he was grinning like a jackass, he unfolded the paper.

Derek,

There is something I need to take care of. Try not to worry.

Please check in on Willa.

I'll be back before you have a chance to miss me.

Ginger xo

Smile fading, a heavy sense of dread settled in the pit of Derek's stomach.

Okay. Okay, relax. She probably just went to the store.

Snatching his phone off the counter, he pressed the speed dial for Ginger's cell. It went straight to voice mail. He swallowed a curse.

Trying valiantly to calm his mounting panic, Derek flung open his apartment door and strode down the hallway. Maybe he'd caught her before she left. *Please* let him have caught her. He took the stairs three at a time, reaching the third floor and her apartment in seconds. The hollow sound of his fist rapping against her door echoed through his skull.

Within seconds, he heard footsteps and the sound of the deadbolt lock turning. His head dropped forward, body deflating with relief. He would shake some sense into Ginger the second the door opened and beg her never to scare him like this again. Bracing his hands on either side of the door, Derek attempted to dial back his panic. He didn't want to start the weekend off by terrifying her.

"Lieutenant. What brings you by this fine evening?"

Derek's head shot up. Patty, the dispatch operator, stood

in the doorway dressed in a fuzzy orange robe and slippers, holding a gossip magazine in her hands. It took him a moment to process her appearance in Ginger's apartment.

"What are you doing here? Where is Ginger?"

"It's wonderful to see you, too."

"Patty, answer me now."

She seemed to realize then that something serious was afoot, because her demeanor went from teasing to businesslike. "I don't know where Ginger is. She called and asked me to hang out here until Willa got home from the dance, and to stay the night. She said I owed her for that stunt I pulled, sending her to the hospital thinking you'd been shot."

Derek tried to breathe, but the air lodged in his chest. "How long have you been here?"

"She left about four hours ago."

"Jesus."

"Is everything okay, Derek?"

"Did she leave you Willa's number?"

Patty didn't take the time to answer, just ducked back in the apartment and returned a moment later holding a slip of paper with Ginger's handwriting on it. It listed his and Willa's numbers along with Lenny's and a short, vague note for Willa, much like his own.

He punched Willa's number in his phone. When she answered, the blast of dance music in the background nearly drowned her voice out completely.

"Where is Ginger?" he demanded. "Did she tell you where she was going?"

"Derek? Wait, hold on. Let me go outside so I can actually hear you."

By the time she came back on the line, Derek's patience had reached a breaking point. His voice reflected the strain. "Willa, think. Do you have any idea where your sister might have gone?"

His tone seemed to give her pause. "No. Isn't she at home?"

Derek paced the hallway like a caged animal. "She's not here. She left me a note saying she had something important to do."

Willa didn't speak for a long moment. "Oh God."

Derek froze, his hand tightening on the phone. "What, goddammit?"

"I can't believe this. I really fucked up."

"Explain. Now."

She dragged in a gulp of breath. "Earlier this week, I was upset over something. I couldn't find Ginger. She wouldn't answer her phone. So I...I called our mother."

Derek's vision blurred around the edges.

"I called her house phone," Willa said quickly. "There's no caller ID. She doesn't know we're in Chicago."

Relief threatened to swamp him, but there had to be more. He could feel the ax above his head, waiting to drop. "Then how exactly did you fuck up, Willa?"

Willa's voice shook as she rambled out the story. "My mother told me Ginger stole some money from her. The night we left. Ginger never told me, but it makes total sense now. Why she snuck me out in the middle of the night."

Derek left behind a gaping Patty, rushing toward his apartment. "And someone back home wants the money back. Is that what your mother told you?"

"Yes," Willa whispered. "Derek, my sister's not a thief. You don't know what it was like—"

He cut her off, already knowing the answer to his question. "*Where. Is. Ginger?*"

"I think she's on her way to Nashville. I know her. Just before I left for the dance, she told me she was going to do the right thing. I didn't know what she was talking about, but it's the money. It has to be." Willa choked on a sob. "Oh God, she doesn't know what's waiting for her down there."

"Shit!" Derek hung up and redialed Ginger's number. He'd planned for every eventuality except Ginger's willfulness. She'd been the wild card all along. And now his carefully laid plan was blowing up in his face. His fist slammed against the wall as he waited for the beep. "Ginger, you turn the goddamn car around right now or I'm coming after you. Call me back *immediately*."

He needed to move. The drive from Chicago to Nashville would take about eight hours and she was already halfway there. Derek hung up the call and grabbed his gun and car keys. Ginger wouldn't turn the car around. He knew it for a fact.

He crumpled the note in his fist and threw it against the wall. Try not to worry? She would be a target the moment she entered Nashville. Valerie knew Ginger had the money. By now, that information had gotten back to Haywood Devon. And Ginger thought she could waltz back into the picture and return what she'd stolen without any consequences?

Re-holstering his gun, Derek hit redial on his cell and waited once more for the beep, closing his eyes at the sound of Ginger's soft drawl. God, he wanted her safe in his arms so bad it physically pained him.

"Baby, listen to me. There are things you don't know. You are walking into a very dangerous situation. Pull over and wait for me, please." He swallowed. "Ginger, I need you. Don't do this."

Derek didn't wait for her to call back, knowing she wouldn't anyway. He took two quick steps toward his desk and picked up the file he'd been building on Haywood Devon over the past week, then slammed out of his apartment.

If he broke the speed limit and got lucky with traffic, he would be in Nashville by morning. Every hour would be critical if he had a shot in hell of saving Ginger.

Chapter Twenty-Four

Peering into the darkened house and deeming it empty, Ginger jiggled the broken window leading to her old bedroom, unsurprised to find it still in disrepair. From her position on the ground, she slid the window as far up as possible, then tossed the canvas sack through the opening. When no one came running, she dragged over an old paint can to boost herself over the sill and climbed inside. The sound of her cowboy boots hitting the floor echoed through the still house and Ginger paused a moment to listen for movement besides her own. Silence greeted her ears.

Glancing around the room, she noted in disgust that Willa's bed still lay unmade from the morning they'd skipped town. Just being in the room made her feel fragile, more vulnerable. In two short weeks, she'd transformed from her previous self. This tiny, airless room was already a distant memory from her past. It made Ginger's skin crawl to remember the things she and Willa had experienced in that very room, so she picked up the bag and walked determinedly through the door leading to the hallway, refusing to dwell on it anymore.

Returning the cash symbolized so much more than doing the honorable thing or being a better role model for Willa. Ginger was doing it for herself, too. As long as she held on to any piece of the past, even in the form of cash, she would never be able to let it go. She'd learned invaluable lessons about human nature inside these four walls, but every decision she made throughout her life couldn't reflect the past or ultimately, it would beat her.

Nothing could beat Ginger, at least not without a fight. Especially now. Love had made her invincible. In a backward way, she supposed, returning the money was her way of moving forward with Derek. She had a feeling he would strongly disagree with her. And if she could gather the courage to listen to his thirty-eight voice mails, she could confirm her theory.

She should've dropped off the money and been halfway back to Chicago by now, but the General, picking a convenient time to surrender, had blown its fan belt outside of Springfield, delaying her for three frustrating hours until the mechanic could complete the repair. She sat in a truck stop diner sipping coffee and studiously ignoring her phone the entire time. It might make her a coward, but she couldn't afford to lose her resolve. Besides, if Derek really wanted her as he'd said, accepting her stubborn nature would be step one.

No, Ginger corrected herself, he *did* want her. She needed to stop thinking in terms of *ifs* and *maybes*. The sooner she stashed the money under Valerie's pillow, the sooner she could get back to Chicago and into his arms to reassure herself of that fact.

The sun began to rise outside, lighting her way into Valerie's bedroom. She hadn't set foot in her mother's room since childhood, afraid of what she would find. She felt little shock at seeing the syringe sitting on the nightstand or the blackened spoon lying next to it. Sighing, she took a step toward the bed.

A car screeched to a stop outside and two doors slammed, followed closely by a third. Two male voices called to each other, but she couldn't make out what they said.

The next closest house was condemned and had been for quite some time, which meant whoever it was had come to see Valerie, or had her mother with them. Ginger's heart accelerated as she ducked behind a chest of drawers. A moment later, the front door opened and crashed against the wall. She covered her mouth and nose with her hand to prevent herself from screaming.

"Where you want her, Haywood?"

A deeper voice spoke. "Anywhere'll do." A heavy object dropped onto the carpet, followed by a slapping noise. "Time to wake up, Valerie. We've got business, you and I."

Ginger's mind raced. Maybe Valerie had passed out somewhere drunk and these men were just bringing her home? Yes, that would be a definite possibility, and not the first or last time it happened. But something about the man's tone sent a warning shivering up her spine.

Valerie groaned.

"That's right. Come on, now. I don't have all day."

"Haywood?" She sounded alarmed. "What do you want?"

He laughed. "You know what I want. I gave you specific instructions: Drop off the package, and bring me back the envelope. Only half of the job got done, so I'm here to remedy that oversight."

"I told you what happened. You should be looking for Ginger. She stole it right out of my goddamn hands while I was sleeping."

"And why were you sleeping, Valerie?" Haywood's voice grew stern. "Perhaps you dipped into the package and took a little product for yourself? You see, I knew you'd have trouble resisting, which is why I told you *no stops* were allowed between the pickup and drop-off."

Without issuing a denial, Valerie started crying. "Well, what are you gonna do?"

"I suppose I'll have to track down this industrious offspring of yours. But first, I'm afraid my associate here will be messing up that face of yours worse than the drugs already have."

Heavy footsteps crossed the carpet, muffling Valerie's sobbing.

Tears rolled down Ginger's cheeks when she heard the first blow. She'd caused this. Whatever Valerie's shortcomings as a mother were, this situation was on Ginger's head. She couldn't stand there and let her mother take a beating for her actions. Furthermore, if this Haywood character succeeded in tracking her down in Chicago, she would lead him straight to Willa. And Derek.

Maybe she could walk out there and give Haywood the money, chalk it up to a big misunderstanding. They'd laugh and toss back a cold one. No harm done.

Unlikely.

Ginger took a deep breath. It was time to end this. She stood and marched into the living room, the bag of money clutched in her hand. "All right, I've got your money. You can stop hitting her now."

Haywood immediately drew his gun, pointing it in her direction. Without flinching, Ginger put both hands in the air, bag and all. She couldn't bring herself to look at her mother, nor could she take her eyes off the gun, but Haywood signaled for the other man to step away from Valerie. Her mother slumped to the floor, choking Ginger with guilt.

Haywood's eyes tracked down her body and he raised an interested eyebrow. With black hair and a goatee, he appeared much younger than his cultured voice indicated. "Well, if I'd known *you* were the thief, I'd have looked for you sooner."

"No need for that now." Ginger tossed the bag onto the floor. "I didn't know who it belonged to and I made a mistake. Take it and leave us be."

His eyes never left hers. "Count it, Winston."

Winston lumbered forward and Ginger shuddered seeing the blood on his knuckles. Her mother's blood. He picked up the bag and dropped it on the couch.

"You think this makes us even? It don't," Valerie slurred. Swallowing, Ginger faced her mother. Face already swelling, her blood-matted hair hung in dull hanks over her eyes. Valerie looked far worse than the last time Ginger saw her, but she could still glimpse the beautiful woman buried beneath prematurely aged skin and sunken eyes, making it twice as tragic.

"I'd have to agree with you there. We're the furthest thing from even."

"I know sarcasm when I hear it." Blood dribbled down her chin. "I know what you two girls think of me. Willa made it clear as crystal over the phone she don't ever want to see me again."

Ginger straightened. "Willa called you? When?"

"Shit, I can't remember. Last month? Yesterday?"

She shook her head. Why hadn't Willa said anything? She looked back at Valerie. Tears tracked down her bloody cheeks, her body shaking with the force of her sobs.

"You know, it ain't easy raising two little babies on your own." She swiped a filthy hand across her cheek. "I was going to get myself together one day, and then twenty-some-odd years came and went before I could blink, you know? It wasn't supposed to be like this."

Suppressing the need to reach out and place a hand on her beaten-down mother's shoulder, Ginger swallowed her sympathy. "Well, it is. It damn well *is* like this, Valerie."

Ginger took one last look at her mother before turning away. Haywood, however, was watching them closely.

"It's short, boss," Winston said from where he sat with the rolls of cash.

Haywood's face pulled into a wide smile. "Short, you say?"

"By twenty-eight hundred."

Ginger's mind raced. *Oh God*, the security deposit on the apartment. She'd completely forgotten. "I can get it for you. Just take me to an ATM and I'll withdraw what's missing." Her checking account could likely cover that amount. She'd barely spent a dime of the money she'd earned at Sensation.

"Sure, that won't be a problem. I'm assuming you can cover the interest as well?"

Her heart sank. "Interest?"

Haywood sauntered toward her, one clammy hand reaching out to caress her cheek. Ginger steeled herself so she wouldn't flinch. "You've put me in a bad position with quite a few people. I can't let that slide."

"How much?" Ginger asked through clenched teeth.

He looked up at the ceiling, as if doings sums in his head. "Oh, double should cover it. That includes the missing amount, plus an extra twenty-eight hundred for my trouble."

Ginger somehow kept the dread from showing on her face. "Fine, drive me to the bank." She didn't have that much cash in her account, but she'd have a better chance of escaping in public.

Haywood laughed as if delighted with her. "I like you. But I also know you don't have that kind of money. Otherwise, you wouldn't have needed to steal mine. No, I think you'll come with me. When your mother brings me the money, you'll be free to go."

She backed away as Winston started coming toward her.

"No. I have the money. You know if you leave it up to her, you'll never see it."

He shrugged. "I'll take my chances. I believe some time with you might prove interesting. And if your mother can't come up with the money, you can always strip in one of my clubs to earn the money."

Disgusted, she spat on his shiny black wing-tip shoe. "Never."

All traces of humor vanished from his eyes. His right hand reared back and slapped Ginger across the face with such stunning force, she stumbled backward. She felt the sting of a cut on her cheek from where his ring had connected with her face.

He signaled his henchman. "Winston?"

Ginger turned and ran. She made it halfway out her bedroom window before Winston wrapped a beefy arm around her waist and dragged her back inside. No matter how hard she struggled, she couldn't break his hold as he dragged her back through the house and out the front door. On the porch, she managed to stomp on his foot with the heel of her boot, but he merely wrapped a hand in her hair, yanking her head back until tears formed in her eyes. He slammed her up against a black sedan, holding her there as he pulled a plastic tie out of his pocket and bound her wrists.

"What are you doing? Untie my wrists. *Please!*" She turned pleading eyes to Haywood, who stood on the porch, arms clasped behind his back. Valerie stood in the doorway behind him smoking a cigarette. "I can get you your money! This is kidnapping!"

A foul-smelling rag cut Ginger off. Winston stuffed it in her mouth and tied it tightly at the back of her head. Then he dragged her toward the trunk. When Ginger saw his intentions, she renewed her struggles, but she wasn't a match for the man's unnatural size. He tossed her into the gigantic trunk. Without her hands to break her fall, the air whooshed from her lungs. She sucked a breath in through her nose, trying to sit up, but he slammed the trunk shut, encapsulating her in darkness.

This can't be happening. No one knew she'd come to Nashville, so she could rule out the possibility of Willa or Derek coming to her aid. Furthermore, there would be a snowstorm in hell before Valerie lifted a finger to help her. It appeared she'd well and truly screwed herself. Ginger pulled her knees up to her chest, attempting to reevaluate. They had to let her out of this trunk at some point. There would be more chances for escape, or if she could just get to a phone—

Tires screeched outside. Several doors slammed. Then she heard the familiar deep pitch of Derek's voice, reinforced by a collection of others. Ginger sprang up, slamming her head against the roof of the trunk. How did he find her? Who else was with him? Trying her best to scream a warning with the obstruction in her mouth, her eyes filled with tears.

Derek, no! They have guns! God, I'm so sorry...

As her voice faded into a dry screech, Ginger fell silent so she could hear what was being said.

"Drop your gun. *Now*. There's ten of us and two of you. We'll put a bullet in both of you before you get a shot off," Derek said.

Ginger heard the faint sound of something heavy sliding through the dirt driveway away from the car. The gun, maybe?

"Well, I certainly recognize our local men in uniform," Haywood said, sounding unhappy about the situation. "But who the hell are *you*?"

"Chicago PD. You don't need to know my name."

Haywood scoffed. "We're a mighty long way from the Windy City. Gentlemen, I recognize quite a few of you as patrons of my various establishments. Why don't we sit down and discuss this without the weapons?"

She heard the click of a gun being cocked. "No can do. I'm the one you'll be dealing with today. They're just here to arrest your sorry ass."

"The woman must be pretty important for all this fanfare. Since when does the Nashville PD send out the cavalry for one white-trash princess?"

Derek's voice turned to ice. "Does the name Thomas Faircourt ring a bell?" Silence from Haywood. "It should. He's your ex-partner. Left Nashville five years ago. And do you know where he ended up?"

A long pause.

"Presently, I have Mr. Faircourt locked up on racketeering charges in Chicago," Derek said. "He was more than happy to cut a deal for less prison time in exchange for information about that little warehouse fire in Nashville about eight years back. The one for which you received the huge insurance settlement. Opened your first strip club with that money, didn't you, Mr. Devon?"

"You're lying. He wouldn't talk."

"I can be very persuasive. Nashville PD was more than happy to assist me today in exchange for the information, seeing as how you've been a thorn in their side for years. Boys?"

Ginger heard the shuffling of feet, some muffled curses, and a struggle, followed by the metallic sound of handcuffs sliding and locking.

A minute later, the trunk popped opened. She stared up into Derek's hard expression and burst into tears. Behind him, several officers marched Haywood and Winston toward a police cruiser. Derek yanked the gag out of her mouth and helped her sit up, turning her face to survey the cut on her cheek.

"Which one of them did this?"

Ginger gulped. He sounded so cold. His touch felt

completely devoid of affection. "H-Haywood."

Derek flipped the gun in his hand and strode toward the cruiser, barking at the officers to wait. Before she could scream for him to stop, he brought the butt of the weapon down on Haywood's skull. The man crumpled to the ground, still handcuffed.

"Now, I hardly see how that was necessary, Lieutenant," an older officer drawled, but his smirk suggested he wasn't overly upset over Haywood's injury.

Ignoring the reprimand, Derek returned to the trunk and slid both arms under Ginger to lift her from the interior. She curled into his hard chest with a sob.

His face devoid of emotion, he placed her in the passenger seat of his SUV, then produced a pocket knife and cut her bonds.

Ginger tried to meet his eyes, but he wouldn't look at her. "Derek—"

"Not a fucking word."

She flinched, sinking back into the seat. It was going to be a long ride back to Chicago.

Chapter Twenty-Five

They rode in silence for an hour, Ginger alternating between contrite and indignant. She wanted to explain her actions to Derek but he stared straight ahead, a muscle ticking ominously in his jaw, effectively preventing conversation. With a sigh, she dug her phone out of her pocket, which Derek had graciously allowed her to retrieve from the truck, and began listening to the numerous voice mails left since yesterday evening.

After Derek's terse initial messages, there were two from Willa begging her to come home. A knot formed in her throat at hearing the fear in her sister's voice. Ginger pressed the speed dial for Willa's cell phone. She answered on the first ring.

"I'm going to kick your ass, Ginger."

"Hey, Wip."

"Not an appropriate time for nicknames."

"I'm sorry. I'm so sorry."

A shuddering sigh. "Are you all right? Is Derek with you?"

"Yeah, he's here. I'm fine."

"Thank fuck. Don't you ever do anything stupid like that again."

She glanced at Derek. "Willa, why didn't you tell me you knew? About the money."

A long sigh. "You know how we operate, Ginger. We don't talk until we're ready. If ever."

"That ends now, okay? No more secrets. We can do better than that."

"Okay." Willa sniffed. "Okay."

Ginger blinked back tears. "I'll be home soon. I want to hear all about the dance."

"Deal."

She hung up and risked another look at Derek. His expression hadn't changed a bit. Punching the button to play her remaining voice mails, Ginger listened to Derek's deep voice in her ear. The first couple messages were filled with palpable anger, but around the tenth voice mail, he turned coaxing and finally resigned. She knew Derek could hear every word from the driver's seat, his body tensing or relaxing at certain points.

"Ginger...I wish you would answer the phone. I really need to hear your voice." A deep, steadying breath. "You know when I fell in love with you?" Ginger's hand tightened on the phone, her pulse hammering. "That night in my bathroom after your apartment flooded. You'd been crying, but you looked so goddamn fearless. Maybe I should have told you how I feel before now. Maybe it would have prevented this fool's mission." He cleared his throat with difficulty. "Probably not. You're too damn stubborn. But then, I love you for that, too, don't I? Call me, sweetheart. I'll come get you and take you home. Bye, baby."

Ginger hung up the phone and stared blindly out the window, cars and buildings whizzing past in a blur. Derek's words repeated themselves over and over in her head. He loved her. But could he forgive her? He couldn't even look her in the eye. Ginger thought of the hard expression on his face when he'd opened the trunk. The way he'd tossed her in his car like a rag doll. Once again, she'd needed his comfort and he didn't provide it. He couldn't just decide to love her then disregard her so quickly, damn him. If he could change his mind about loving her so easily, she could surely reverse it back in her favor, right?

Derek veered off the highway onto an exit ramp, turned at the first light, and pulled into a motel parking lot.

"Why are we stopping?"

"Because I haven't showered or slept in three days and I need to do both before driving any farther."

Ginger's eyes traced over his heavily stubbled jaw and dark-circled eyes. Her heart tripped over itself at the fatigue she saw there. Before she could offer to take the wheel, he climbed out of the vehicle, strode into the motel office, and returned a few minutes later with a room key.

He jerked open her passenger side door and waited for Ginger to slide out, then grabbed a leather gym bag from the backseat.

Once they reached their room, Derek locked the door behind them and removed his shirt. In the dim light filtering through the window, shadows played against his muscular chest and back. Black dress pants hung low on his hips, but soon he removed those, too.

Ginger sank onto the bed and tried to sift through the conflicting emotions roiling inside of her. Anger warred with pain. Guilt simmered beneath the ever-present desire she felt around Derek. He was treating her like one of his subordinates and she hated him for it. Why couldn't he just talk to her, order her around—something?

"Take off your clothes," he directed without turning

around.

Okay scratch that, she *so* wasn't in the mood to be ordered around. Ginger scoffed. "Not a chance."

"I would remove them *for* you, but I can't ensure they'll remain intact."

Hating the hollow quality to his voice, she rose from the bed and stomped toward him. "Derek, you've had your time to be mad. I did something foolish, I know that. But you can't ignore me forever."

He moved so fast, Ginger didn't have time to protest as Derek ripped the shirt from her body. Her shorts were yanked down her legs next, along with her panties. Then he threw her over his shoulder and strode into the bathroom. The light flipped on so she could see herself in the mirror dangling over his back.

"What are you doing? Are you crazy?"

"I'm taking a goddamn shower. I don't trust you to stay put, so you're taking one with me. Would you like to remove your boots or will they be joining us?"

Having no choice, Ginger frantically toed her boots off and let them drop to the ground. She heard the shower start, then a moment later he stepped under the spray. The warm water rushed over her, soaking her bra and running down into her eyes. Finally, Derek bent and set her down on her feet.

She launched herself at him, pummeling his wet chest with her fists. He absorbed the blows without reaction, not even trying to prevent her.

"Why don't you just get it over with?" Ginger cried through gritted teeth. "Punish me. You know you want to."

Derek's eyes darkened and his fists clenched, letting Ginger know she'd hit her mark. She removed her bra and stepped under the shower spray, letting him get an eyeful of the water rushing over her naked body. Then she turned and placed her palms high against the tile wall.

"Punish me."

A tortured groan echoed through the bathroom. "*No*, Ginger. You don't know what I'm capable of right now."

"You need it."

"Don't tell me what I need," he growled into her wet hair. "You've made it clear how little you care."

Her throat squeezed at the pain behind his words, but she pushed on. "I need it, too. We'll both feel better afterward."

Breath harsh against her ear, Derek pressed against her back. "You would like that, wouldn't you? A spanking followed by a long, wet ride on my dick?"

"Yes. Yes, *please*, Derek." Arching her back, Ginger pressed her behind against his slippery arousal, working her hips, enticing him to follow through. She made a sound of protest when his fingers dug into her waist to still her movements.

"Too bad, baby. It's not punishment when you enjoy the sentence. No, I have something far worse in store for you."

Derek picked up a bar of soap wrapped in paper, ripping it open with his teeth as Ginger watched over her shoulder. Then he lathered the bar in his hand and began to wash her. Gently, his hands ran over her back, across her belly, dipping between her legs just long enough to frustrate her. He gathered her hair in one hand and pulled it over her shoulder so he could wash the blood from her face. Ginger's hands slipped from the wall and she swayed back toward him unconsciously, greedy for his touch.

"Wh-what are you doing?"

"I saw your face in the car, Ginger." His voice sounded low, furious. "When you heard that message. You looked terrified."

She shook her head in denial. "No, I—"

"*Yes.* So you know what your punishment is going to be,

sweetheart? I'm going to make *love* to you. Slowly. Hell, it might take me until tomorrow. I'm going to lose count of how many times you come. And every time you do, I'm going to tell you that I love you. Until you fucking get used to it."

Tears burned behind her eyes. God, he sounded so hurt. She turned to face him. "Derek, listen to me—"

"No." His throat worked with emotion. "You're not going to cry your way out of this."

Ginger knew then she wouldn't get through to him with words, only actions. They'd admitted to being physical people since the beginning. Only her body could persuade him to listen. As the water pounded around them, she put her hands on either side of his face and stared deep into his eyes. She stretched up to place her mouth on his and felt a stab of pain in her chest when he flinched.

Garnering her courage, she poured every ounce of love she held for him into the kiss. She apologized with her mouth for making him scared. She praised him for saving her life. Her hands stroked his face and neck, dipping down to his shoulders to pull him closer. Derek's arousal pulsed hard and thick between them, but she didn't reach for it like she wanted to, worried he might mistake her meaning. The kiss represented love and she needed him to understand that.

Derek pulled away to scrutinize her face. "Ginger?"

Tears mixing with spray from the shower, she nodded. "I love you, too."

His eyes squeezed shut. Banding her arms around his waist, she buried her face against his skin and repeated the words over and over again, willing him to believe her.

She heard the shower turn off. Then Derek lifted her in his arms and carried her out of the bathroom. Laying her down, still soaking wet, on the pillows of the bed, Derek sat heavily with his back to her and buried his head in his hands. Propping herself up on her elbow, she waited without breathing.

When he finally spoke, his voice sounded hoarse. "When I turned the corner into your mother's driveway, all I saw was that man tossing you into the trunk and slamming the lid. I couldn't tell if you were alive or..." Ginger scrambled onto her knees, wrapping herself around him from behind. "When I heard you yelling and kicking, I think it might have been the most beautiful sound I've ever heard."

Ginger pressed her face into his damp neck. "I'm sorry. I'm sorry I scared you."

Derek remained quiet for a moment. "I know I'm overprotective, but there's a good reason for it. I see a lot of terrible things in my job, Ginger. Murders. The entire drive to Nashville, I couldn't stop picturing your face on every single one..."

She climbed around him and onto his lap, forcing him to look at her. "Stop. Don't think about it anymore. I'm right here. I'll never do anything like that again."

"You're goddamn right you won't."

His gruffness made her smile, but it wavered under the importance of her next question. "And about taking that money...you don't think less of me for that?"

Derek was already shaking his head. "Never. Especially after seeing where you grew up. And meeting Valerie."

She bit her lip. "I suppose the worst way to introduce your boyfriend to your mother is from inside a trunk."

"Please. I'm not ready to think about that again." Uncertain eyes searched hers. "When you heard the voice mail...that look on your face..."

"Oh." She blew out a shaky breath and tried to climb off his lap. Derek merely tightened his hold. "I thought maybe after what I'd done, you would change your mind. Decide I was too much trouble."

Before the words were out of her mouth, Ginger found

herself flat on her back with Derek looming above her. "Change my mind?" He sounded incredulous. "Ginger, I don't want to encourage you to attempt anything like this ever again, let me make that *abundantly* clear. But I would come after you every time. *Every. Time.*"

Ginger laughed through her tears, but it turned into a moan when Derek parted her thighs and thrust deep inside her, holding her still against the mattress.

"Look at me. You own me. I'm *owned*." He shifted his hips, making her whimper. "You own this, too."

She moved restlessly beneath him. "Oh, Derek…please."

Leaning down, he kissed her lips sweetly. "Easy, baby. I meant what I said. I want to make love to you. Let me, beautiful girl."

Entwining his fingers with hers, Derek started to move.

Epilogue

"You're not bringing that thing into our bedroom."

"That *thing*?"

"You heard me. It gives me the creeps. Do you know how hard it is to creep out someone who investigates homicide for a living?"

"A harmless statue?"

Derek confirmed with a single nod, shivering as Ginger wheeled Dolly through the living room. She merely rolled her eyes. After ten months of pretending to live separately, yet spending every single night together, Ginger had finally consented to move in with him. Having tired of her stall tactics, albeit adorable, Derek decided to play dirty, demanding her agreement one night while her legs were up near her ears.

Since then, he'd had to fight to keep the constant smile off his face. She already had him wrapped around her little finger, he didn't need to give her another reason to torture him.

"Think of it this way, baby. I won't be able to get hard with a toothy blonde staring down at me."

Ginger propped a hand on her hip and pouted, heating his blood. "I seem to recall you used to prefer toothy blondes."

Derek growled, starting toward her. She knew her jealousy turned him on. Big time. Squealing, she turned and ran barefoot into their bedroom. Of course, he chased her. He would always chase her.

He tackled her on the bed, tickling her sides.

"Stop! Oh my God, stop *stop*."

Her shirt rode up, revealing her navel. Dipping his head, Derek circled her belly button with his tongue. When Ginger's fingers curled into his recently grown-out hair, tugging with encouragement, he smiled against her belly. Growing his hair out had been a great decision, even if it was a pain in the ass every morning.

"Derek, we can't. Willa and Evan will be here any minute."

He groaned, rolling onto his back, only slightly appeased when she continued playing with his hair. "So Willa is staying here and Evan is staying in your old apartment?"

Ginger laughed. "No. They're both staying in the old apartment. They're grown-ups now. And they *have* been studying abroad in Italy for the last three months."

Derek frowned. "I guess I still think of her as a kid."

"I know. And it's very sweet how protective you are of my sister." She tugged on a fistful of hair. "In fact, it's kind of a turn-on."

Derek's eyebrows shot up. "Another one? Jesus, how many do you have?"

"I don't know. You keep discovering them."

He turned onto his stomach and crawled up Ginger's body, his eyes focused on her mouth. "Are you sure we don't have time?"

Her breath turned shallow. "Be quick."

His fingers flew to the button of her shorts.

The doorbell rang.

"*Fuck*." They groaned at the same time.

But Ginger's lips spread into a smile as she bounded off the bed. Three months was the longest amount of time she'd ever spent apart from Willa. Derek knew she missed her sister terribly. The end of Willa's semester abroad coincided perfectly with the grand opening of Ginger's new furniture store, Sneaky Peet's. They'd spent the last two weeks painting and transporting her inventory to the space in Wicker Park. Several local papers were already creating a buzz about the trendy new store. Derek had every faith that the shop would be successful with Ginger running the show.

"Baby, wait."

At the bedroom door, she turned with one hand on the doorjamb, eyes shining with excitement. All bare legs and tousled hair, she knocked the breath out of him. Still did every single day.

"Yes, Lieutenant?"

He smiled, then turned serious. "You're moving in today. Do you know how happy that makes me?"

Ginger launched herself at him, knocking them backward onto the bed. Straddling his chest, she leaned down and kissed him the way Derek asked her to when he needed reassurance. The way she'd done ten months ago in that motel shower when he needed it most. A kiss that didn't require words.

Another round of banging on the door.

"Mommy and Daddy!" Willa called from the hallway. "Zip up your pants and open the door."

Ginger kissed him one last time and ran from the bedroom laughing.

Acknowledgments

To my husband, Patrick, who in addition to working incredibly hard himself, never complains about having to watch the baby while I write (or just sob quietly in a corner wishing I'd never quit smoking). You're more than I deserve.

To Heather Howland for taking a chance with a new author and being patient throughout this unfamiliar, whirlwind process.

To my mother, father, and brother, who *better* not be reading a word of this book. I love you so much. Thank you for your understanding.

A special thanks to my friend Maggie (aka "Robin") who read my very first manuscript three times and insisted it was totally amazing when in reality, it was horrific.

And to my ladies! The funniest, craziest girls on the island of Manhattan whose real-life adventures inspire all the female relationships I write about. Best night of my life!

About the Author

NYT and *USA TODAY* bestselling author Tessa Bailey lives in Brooklyn, New York, with her husband and young daughter. When she isn't writing or reading romance, she enjoys a good argument and thirty-minute recipes.

www.tessabailey.com
Join Bailey's Babes!

Discover the rest of the **Line of Duty** *series...*

HIS RISK TO TAKE

OFFICER OFF LIMITS

PROTECTING WHAT'S THIERS

ASKING FOR TROUBLE

STAKING HIS CLAIM

Also by Tessa Bailey...

UNFIXABLE
a New Adult novel featuring Willa from
Protecting What's His

RISKIER BUSINESS

RISKING IT ALL

UP IN SMOKE

BOILING POINT

RAW REDEMPTION

OWNED BY FATE

EXPOSED BY FATE

DRIVEN BY FATE

CRASHED OUT

THROWN DOWN

WORKED UP

WOUND TIGHT

BAITING THE MAID OF HONOR

Enjoy more heat from Entangled…

ONE NIGHT STAND AFTER ANOTHER
a novel by Amanda Usen

Clara Duke lives to crochet wearable art. But right this second, she's looking at the one guy who has the uncanny ability to unravel her in every possible way. *Zane Brampton.* A whole night with this delectable, gorgeous man would be nothing less than a total sexpocalypse. But then Zane wants his chance to prove he deserves more than one night…and he might just be the thread that snaps all of Clara's perfectly crocheted plans.

UNDERCOVER ENGAGEMENT
a Private Pleasures novel by Samanthe Beck

By-the-book Eden Brixton is not happy about being assigned to an undercover op with wild-card Markus Swain. Pretending to be engaged and all the hot, steamy chemistry that comes with it will be next to impossible. Or so Marcus believes, until Eden knocks him on his ass with temptation he can't resist. But when the heat gets too real, it becomes clear doing the op might prove to be their undoing.

HIS HOLIDAY CRUSH
a novel by Cari Z

One meeting away from making partner, Max Robertson is guilted into coming back home for Christmas. The plan is to go for just one night, but a wild deer and a snow bank wreck everything. Former Army Sergeant Dominic Bell of the Edgewood police has his evening turned upside-down when he gets called out to a crash—and it's his one and only high school crush. Everyone deserves a present this holiday season, right?

LIKE A BOSS
an Accidentally Viral novel by Anne Harper

As if it wasn't bad enough that her long-term boyfriend dumped her, Nell Bennett goes viral online for ranting in a restaurant about her perpetually single status. Thankfully a kind and attractive stranger offers to share his table with her…and their sizzling banter leads to a surprising kiss before they part ways. Now her tiny hometown of Arbor Bay is buzzing over their latest Internet celebrity, but Nell's no stranger to attention. Still, even she never expected to show up to work only to discover her brand-new boss is a very familiar face…